EVER-GREENE
A Souls Christmas

ANNABELLA
MICHAELS

DEDICATION

This book is dedicated to my husband. Of all the
Christmases I've had and all the Christmases yet
to come, there is no one I'd rather spend them with
than you. You are my best friend, the love of my life
and my soulmate.

EVER-GREENE
A Souls Christmas

CHAPTER
One

Caleb

I PULLED INTO THE DRIVEWAY AND SMILED WHEN I saw the lights on inside the house. I'd ended up staying later at the restaurant than I'd expected because I had to finish filling out a supply order. With Christmas just a week away, I knew the suppliers would be shutting down for several days. So, as much as I wanted to hurry home, I'd had no choice but to stay late and get it done.

I loved being a chef and running Romero's with my husband, Giovanni, but there was nothing better in the world than being home with him and our daughter, Sarah. Those were the moments I lived for, when it was just the three of us, watching a movie, eating dinner, or reading books together.

I parked the car and grabbed the bag from the seat next to me. The wind was howling when I opened the door and it hit me in the face like an icy blast. I'd grown up in Chicago, but sometimes, I was still taken by surprise at how frigid it could get in the winter. The local meteorologists were predicting we'd have a white Christmas and I hoped they were right.

Most people thought I was crazy when I told them I loved snow, but I'd always enjoyed it. Some of my favorite memories were of me, my brothers, and sisters going sledding down the big hill in our backyard. Mom would bundle us up in so many layers of clothes that it was surprising we could still walk, and then we'd spend all day racing down the hill with the snow and wind in our faces.

Mom would call for us to come inside and despite the fact that we could no longer feel our bodies, we still always tried to argue that we weren't cold. She would insist though and there would be hot chocolate with miniature marshmallows on top and a plate full of Christmas cookies waiting for us in the kitchen. They were great memories and I wanted my daughter to grow up experiencing that same kind of carefree joy.

I stepped into our home and sighed gratefully when I saw that Gio had started a fire in the fireplace. I set the bag down on the small entryway table and hung my coat up in the hall closet, laying my shoes inside there as well so I wouldn't track any dirt into the house. I walked over to the fire and spread my hands out in front of it to warm them.

I thawed out after a minute or two, then took off in search of my husband and little girl. I smiled when I reached the top of the stairs and heard Sarah's uninhibited peals of laughter. I followed the sounds and found her in the bathtub, laughing hysterically as she gazed up at her daddy who sat on the floor next to the tub. I couldn't see what he was doing because his back was to me, but whatever it was, it was obviously very funny.

I leaned against the doorframe and crossed my arms as I watched them interact with each other. Gio had dreamed of being a father for years and I'd always imagined he'd be a good one, but nothing could've prepared me for the reality of watching him be a father to Sarah.

From the moment the little four-year-old came into our lives, Gio had been putty in her hands. Of course, he often said the same about me, which I would have to admit was true. Sarah had come to us when the adoption agency had contacted us about a little girl who they were having trouble finding a permanent home for because people were leery about taking on the responsibility of caring for a child with Down syndrome. We agreed to meet her and when they brought Sarah into the room, Gio and I had looked at each other, tears welling up in our eyes. We'd known right away that she was meant to be our daughter. We started the adoption process immediately and soon we were able to bring Sarah home to live with us, becoming a family.

"Dad!" Sarah said as she pointed in my direction. My heart melted at the excited look on her face as she saw me.

"Hey, baby girl! Are you getting a bath?" I asked as I stepped into the bathroom.

Sarah nodded her head and Gio turned around to face me. As soon as I saw his face, I realized why Sarah had been laughing so hard and I found myself chuckling too. Giovanni had a full beard of bubbles on his chin and a dollop on his nose. He looked utterly ridiculous and beautiful at the same time, and my heart tripped all over itself at how in love with him I was.

"Hey, baby, welcome home," Gio said with a happy grin. I bent down and gave him a kiss, not caring that I was getting a face full of bubbles. I'd been away from him all day and I wanted to feel him as close to me as possible. Of course, what I wanted most would have to wait until after we put Sarah to bed. Gio winked at me as if he knew what I'd been thinking, and I felt my face heat as I stood back up to grab a couple of towels from the linen closet.

"There's that blush I love so much," he said quietly as I handed him one of the towels.

He made sure to brush his fingers over mine as he reached for it and a thrill traveled up my arm and throughout the rest of my body. I used to wonder if some of the passion—the desperate need—I had for him, would fade once the newness of our relationship wore off, but instead, it had only grown the more time we spent together. I honestly couldn't imagine that there would ever come a day when my body wouldn't react to his that way. The man just did it for me.

Gio wiped the bubbles from his face and then began draining the tub while I hauled a wet and squirming Sarah out of the water and wrapped a towel around her. I kissed the tip of her nose as I ran the towel over her hair and she giggled. I sighed happily. Sometimes, I still couldn't believe how perfect my life had turned out. I was married to the most wonderful and sexy man, we had a daughter that was loving and sweet, I had an amazing family, and spent my days working a job I loved. *Life just doesn't get any better than this.*

"How about I take this little cutie and get her ready for bed while you change," Gio offered, holding his arms out for Sarah and making a silly face at her which made her giggle.

"Thank you," I said gratefully. "I'll be in soon to help tuck her in."

I went to our room and pulled a pair of pajama pants and a soft t-shirt out of the dresser and started unbuttoning my shirt. I could hear Gio and Sarah over the baby monitor we kept in our room in case she ever needed us in the middle of the night. The sounds of him blowing a raspberry somewhere on her and Sarah's high-pitched squeals in response had me grinning. I hurried when I heard him start to read her a bedtime story, not wanting to miss telling her goodnight before she fell asleep.

I walked across the hall to her room and found Gio in the rocking chair. Sarah was sitting in his lap with her thumb in her mouth as he read *Chicka Chicka Boom Boom*. Gio smiled at me as I walked in and sat down on the floor in front of them, never stopping the steady cadence of his voice. My gaze traveled back and forth between the two people who owned my heart so completely.

Sarah's eyes grew heavy and she leaned her head on Gio's chest. Within minutes she was sound asleep, and he shut the book, handing it to me as he stood from the chair while cradling our daughter in his arms. I kissed her cheek gently, so I wouldn't wake her, and then Gio laid her down, kissing her forehead and raising the rails along the side of the bed so she wouldn't roll out and hurt herself. I covered her with a blanket and then followed my husband out of the room, switching the light off as I went. We made our way down the stairs quietly.

"I brought dinner home from the restaurant," I told him, grabbing the bag of food from where I'd left it near the front door.

"Mmm. That sounds great," Gio answered as we walked into the kitchen.

"You don't even know what I brought," I said with a chuckle.

"I like everything you make so it doesn't really matter what it is," he responded with a shrug.

I pulled him towards me and kissed him then whispered in his ear. "You are going to get so lucky for that comment." My tongue flicked out, tracing the shell of his ear.

Gio leaned back so he could see my face. His eyes darkened considerably, and I felt his breath fan against my skin as he spoke. "There's suddenly something I want more than food."

"Oh, what is that?" I asked coyly.

"You," he answered, slamming his lips over mine.

He coaxed my mouth open with his own and I moaned when his tongue swept inside, brushing against mine and licking at the roof as if it were the first time and he wanted to explore every inch of me.

My hands gripped his broad shoulders as I felt myself begin to sway. His hands came down and cupped my ass, his touch burning me through the thin material of my pajamas. I tilted my head back as he licked a path down my neck, stopping to suck on the tender flesh where my neck met my shoulder. Gio had always liked to mark me, staking his claim on me.

There had been a brief time when he had ended things and it had hurt to see the marks he'd left behind. They'd served as a reminder of everything I had lost, but we made it through that rough patch and were stronger than ever. Now, when he marked me, it was a reminder of our love and the passion between us, and it filled me with a sense of pride.

"I need you, little one," Gio said, pulling my shirt over my head and dropping it to the floor. My heart raced when I heard the special name he used only for me.

"I'm all yours," I told him, my voice coming out breathy and full of need.

He growled low, the sound rumbling up from his chest. He obviously liked my answer because he didn't waste any time as he pulled me closer. I sucked in a breath when my aching cock brushed deliciously against his body as he lifted me. My arms slid around his broad shoulders and I locked my legs around his waist as he carried me from the kitchen into the living room.

Gio laid me down on the rug in front of the fire then brushed the hair off my forehead as he stared down at me. I gazed up at him and was met with so much love and adoration in his eyes that it literally took my breath away. I swallowed hard past the lump in my throat as my emotions threatened to choke me with their intensity.

"Do you have any idea how much I love you?" he whispered. His fingers brushed down the side of my face and his thumb grazed my bottom lip. My tongue flicked out to lick it and he hissed between his teeth in response.

"Show me," I demanded. I knew this man better than anyone else in the world. I knew who his heart belonged to because he told me every day in a million different ways, but right then, I didn't want any more words; instead, I wanted our bodies to speak for us.

We quickly divested ourselves of our clothes until we lay naked, Gio's hips nestled between my legs, his body covering mine. He kissed me deeply while his cock rubbed up and down alongside mine, igniting the flames inside me until I was sure my body was running hotter than the fire beside us.

He licked his way down my neck until he reached one of my nipples and then he latched on, sucking it hard, in the way he knew drove me insane. My hips punched up off the floor and I cried out as electricity shot through my body. His tongue swirled over the rigid nub, soothing the sting away as his hand traveled lower until it circled my cock.

My breaths came in short puffs as he continued to move further south, his fist gripping me as it slid up and down my length. Pre-cum flowed from my tip like a leaky faucet, coating his fingers and increasing the ease of the glide. He kissed his way across my stomach and stopped to let his tongue dip and swirl inside my navel.

I reached down and gripped his hair in my hands, guiding him to where I so desperately wanted to feel his touch. As always, Gio gave me exactly what I wanted. He sucked the head of my cock between his full lips and moaned as my juices coated his tongue.

As if my flavor had flipped a switch inside him, he began sucking me with wild abandon. His head lowered further down my shaft, his wet heat engulfing me all the way to the root. He held my cock in the tight channel of his throat and swallowed at the same time his finger, slick with pre-cum, slid inside my body.

"Gio!" I gasped as he increased his suction, his finger thrusting in and out of me until I was out of my mind with desire. "Please, Gio. I can't wait. I need you, now," I begged.

His lips were red and swollen and glistening in the firelight as he rose to his knees. His eyes never left mine, not even when he reached into the drawer on the coffee table and pulled out a bottle of lube. I heard the click of the cap and he poured some onto his fingers. I spread my legs wide for him as he stared down at me hungrily.

"I will never get tired of seeing you like this; naked, vulnerable, exposed. Knowing that I'm the only one who gets to see you like this, that you're all mine. It awakens something in me that I'm not sure I can hold back," he rasped.

"Then don't. I never want you to hold back with me. You're mine and I want every single thing you have to give, Gio," I told him.

He stared at me for a long moment as if testing the weight of my words and then he slicked his cock and lined it up with my hole. He hesitated for a second and I opened my mouth to speak, but then his hips punched forward, and he drove into me, smoothly, perfectly, as if our bodies were made for one another. He leaned down and covered my mouth with his own, effectively swallowing my scream so we wouldn't wake Sarah.

He held still, allowing me time to adjust to the size of him, but I didn't need that. My body recognized his like we were two perfectly matched puzzle pieces. I reached my hands down and palmed the round globes of his ass, gripping them and pulling him forward. He slid in the rest of the way until his hips were pressed snugly against my ass.

"Don't hold back," I demanded. Gio stared down at me with a fierce expression and then he reached above my head and grabbed one of the throw pillows which had fallen off the couch. He handed it to me and I gave him a puzzled look.

"When you need to scream, *bite it*," he growled.

My eyes widened, and I almost came right there, but then I was too busy following his instructions as he latched his arms around my thighs and lifted my hips off the floor. With my legs locked tightly around his waist and my ass in the air, I was completely at his mercy. He could do whatever he wanted to me while I was expected to just go along for the ride and *I. Loved. It.*

His hips thrust forward, and the head of his cock grazed that exquisite spot inside me. I bit down on the corner of the pillow, muffling my screams as he pulled back out, awakening every nerve along the way. His fingers dug into my skin as his hips continued to punch forward, pegging my prostate with perfect accuracy every time. Sweat dripped from his forehead and landed on my stomach as he bent forward to watch my body swallow his cock.

I reached for my dick and began stroking as my orgasm built inside me. My wrist flicked faster as his hips plunged harder and deeper with every thrust. I could feel the telltale tingling at the base of my spine and I looked at him desperately.

"I'm right there. Come for me, baby," he commanded through clenched teeth.

He didn't have to tell me again. My eyes rolled up into the back of my head and I screamed into the pillow as cum shot from the tip of my cock, splashing over my chest and landing on my neck. I was lost in a sea of bliss and barely registered Gio's low growl, the cords in his neck straining as he came, filling me with his hot seed.

I threw the pillow aside as he collapsed on top of me and wrapped my arms around him as we both floated, our staggered breaths mingling with each other. We kissed, clinging to each other as the aftershocks of our love rippled through us, making us tremble.

"That was amazing. I swear, it gets better and better every time we make love," he whispered.

"It's because I keep falling more and more in love with you every day," I told him with a sated grin. It was the truth, the deeper our commitment to each other became, the better everything was between us.

After a few minutes, Gio moved to lie on the floor and pulled me to his side. I lay my head on his chest, curling an arm and a leg over top of him, possessively. The warmth of the fire and the sound of his heart beating steadily beneath my cheek lulled me into a peaceful state and my eyes grew heavy.

"How was your day?" he asked, pulling me from

my sleepiness. His fingers sifted through my hair and I tilted my head to look at him with a smile, suddenly remembering what I had been looking forward to telling him.

"It was great! Curtis got back today, and he said he'd be happy to cover for me over the holidays," I said. Gio's eyes lit up as he smiled.

"Did he and Jakob have a good time in Hawaii?" he asked.

"It's Hawaii and they were on their honeymoon, what's not to love?" I rolled my eyes teasingly. Gio chuckled and I felt it vibrate through his chest.

"I'm glad they had a good time and I'm so happy we'll be able to spend time with our family without worrying about the restaurant. This is our first Christmas with Sarah and I want to enjoy every second of it," he said, his smile widening.

"Yeah," I said with a happy sigh. "I can't wait to show you and Sarah what a traditional Greene family Christmas was like when I was a kid."

"I'm sure we'll love it. But first, I need some food," Gio said with a grin. I laughed when I heard his stomach growl and I sat up, pulling him along with me.

"Come on, big guy. I think we've both built up quite an appetite."

CHAPTER
Two

Micah

"I'M TELLING YOU GUYS, I'VE NEVER SEEN anything like it," Carlos told us as he shook his head. "I've guarded a few celebrities since I started working here, but that lady took the cake."

"Oh, come on. You had a cushy gig, following around a supermodel while she was in town. How hard could it be to watch over her and make sure she didn't break a nail?" Greg joked.

"Trust me, I would have rather been assigned to a mob boss," Carlos told him. "She was extremely demanding and rude to everyone around her and if that weren't bad enough, she expected me to take care of her dog. At least, I think it was a dog, it looked more like a rat to me."

As a former Green Beret, I knew Carlos had dealt with much worse than a tiny dog, so the horrified expression on his face made me laugh, and Brandon and Greg joined in. I looked around at the men gathered in the conference room with a smile. There were a few others who worked for me, but were out of the office at the moment. Each one of them were former military Special Forces and had been carefully selected to work at my firm, Hamilton Security, because they were the best in their respective fields.

Even though we'd served in different branches of the military, we'd become brothers in our own right, and I trusted each and every one of them with my life. In fact, I'd trusted them with something even more important than my life, in my opinion. I'd trusted them to keep my family safe.

I'd grown up without much family to speak of before moving in with my best friend, Giovanni, and his parents for a short while. G's parents had taught me what family was all about, but when they'd died, I assumed I'd never know that feeling again.

Then I met and fell in love with Landon and I

was suddenly thrown into a loud, boisterous, and at times, crazy family, and I had never been happier. They welcomed me into their circle and accepted me as one of their own. I loved the Greenes with my whole heart and I was fiercely protective of them.

My head turned as the door swung open and my smile grew when I saw Mary walk in. I may have been the owner of Hamilton Security, but everyone who worked there knew that it was Mary who was in charge. She ran my office like a tight ship, not taking flak from anyone, yet fiercely protective of "her boys." We'd taken to calling her Southern Mama, not only because of her Tennessee roots, but the way she took care of each of us as if we were her own children. I, along with every other guy who worked there, adored her.

"You have a phone call, Micah," she told me.

"Thanks, Mary." I looked around the table at the other men. "I think we're done here unless you guys have anything else." When they shook their heads, I stood and followed Mary out the door.

"It's Mr. Jackson. He wants an update on his son. He's on line two," she said.

"Thank you, I'll take it in my office." I made my way down the hallway and shut the door behind me, so I'd have some privacy.

A few hours later, I pushed my chair away from my desk and stood with a sigh, stretching my arms over my head to work the stiffness out of my body from sitting for so long. Desk work was my least favorite part of the job. I'd much prefer to be out in the field, but it was a necessary part of owning a business. I quickly straightened my desk then walked out to the main reception area where I found Mary and Greg talking.

"I'm heading out. Call me if you need anything," I told her, stopping at her desk as I slid my coat on and wrapped my scarf around my neck.

"Got a hot date tonight?" Greg asked.

"You've seen my husband. My date is the hottest in the world," I bragged.

"I still don't get how you got a guy like Landon to fall for your ugly mug," he teased.

"I don't know either, but now that I've got him, I'm never letting him go," I assured him with a smile.

"I think they're lucky to have each other. Give Landon my love," Mary told me.

"Will do. You guys have a great night and call me if you need anything." With a wave over my shoulder, I walked out the front door. The air was crisp, and I could see my breath as I walked across the parking lot to my Jeep. I climbed inside and cranked the heat then sent Landon a text as I waited for the windows to defrost.

Me: Leaving work. Be home soon.

It only took a second for his response to come through.

Landon: Hurry! I've missed you.

I smiled as I slid my phone in my pocket and backed out of my parking space. Before Landon, I never thought I'd be the type that would enjoy being in a relationship, but he changed all that. Landon was everything that was good and right in an otherwise crazy world and he made me feel happier whenever I was near him. He was exactly the person I never knew I was looking for and I loved him more than I ever thought possible.

It didn't take long before I was pulling up to the home that Landon and I shared together. The wind whipped at my cheeks and I tucked my chin down into my scarf for warmth as I rushed up the stairs and through the front door. I hung my coat and scarf up and headed into the kitchen where I could hear Landon moving around.

I grinned when I walked in and found him standing at the stove, his hips swaying back and forth as he stirred something in a pan. Perry Como was crooning through the speakers about there being no place like home for the holidays and I couldn't have agreed more. Anywhere that Landon was, was home to me. I moved in behind my gorgeous husband and placed my hands on his hips. He jumped at first when he realized he wasn't alone, but then he leaned his body into mine and looked at me over his shoulder.

"Hey, baby!" he said, his face lighting up with his smile. His hazel eyes were soft, and I could see the love he felt for me shining in their depths as he offered me his lips. I leaned in, capturing his mouth with my own and groaned as his tongue swept over mine. He tasted sweet and delicious; all Landon and all mine.

"What are you making?" I asked, ending the kiss and leaning my chin on his shoulder. I took a deep breath, letting Landon's scent erase the stress of a long workday. Having my husband near always helped calm me.

"It's the sauce for the chicken I baked," he answered.

"It smells delicious," I said, placing kisses along the side of his neck. "But not as delicious as you. What do you say we put all this in the oven to keep it warm and go in the bedroom for a while?"

I could feel Landon's body melt against mine as I

licked over the shell of his ear and his head dropped back to land on my shoulder. I reached around to the front of him and ran my hand over the prominent bulge in his pants. He shivered in my arms and I smiled as I heard his breathing increase. My hands reached for his belt, but he stopped me before I could get it undone. His pupils were blown wide when he turned to face me, and I bent my head for another taste, but he surprised me by stepping to the side and out of my arms.

"Where are you going?" I asked, trying to keep the disappointment out of my voice. I knew I'd failed when I saw Landon's lips lift up in a knowing smirk.

"As much as I want that, and you *know*, I want that, we don't have time," he explained.

"What do you mean we don't have time?" I asked just as the doorbell rang. I glanced towards the front door and then back at Landon.

"Morgan and Akio are coming over for dinner, remember?" he said, giving me an apologetic smile.

"Now, I do," I murmured, glancing down. I'd been so focused on my sexy husband that I hadn't even noticed the table set for four.

"Later," Landon promised, reaching for my hand. He pulled me in and gave me a quick kiss.

"I'm holding you to that," I growled.

Morgan and Akio stood on the front porch, grinning at us as we opened the door and despite my frustration at the turn of events, I found myself smiling back. Morgan was Landon's favorite cousin and his husband, Akio, was Landon's best friend. They were both incredible people and I enjoyed spending time with them whenever we were able to.

"Hey, guys! Come in," I offered, holding the door for them.

"Thanks, it's freezing out there," Morgan said as he stepped inside.

"Oh, man! It smells great in here." Akio sniffed at the air as I took their coats and hung them in the closet.

"Good, I hope you're hungry," Landon said as he led our guests to the kitchen.

I handed Morgan a bottle of wine to pour while I helped Landon transfer all the food onto serving dishes. Landon was a great cook, having picked up some tips from Caleb over the years and he'd clearly outdone himself with citrus chicken baked to perfection, roasted red potatoes, and fresh green beans with slivered almonds.

"This looks amazing, baby." I kissed his cheek as he handed me a bowl.

"Thank you," Landon said quietly, blushing

slightly. I stared at him for a moment, completely enraptured by how beautiful he was, inside and out. I knew how lucky I was to have him in my life and my heart felt like it was going to burst with how much I loved him.

"Wow! I thought *we* were bad," I heard Akio say in a stage whisper. I turned to look at the two other men that I had momentarily forgotten were in the room and found them wearing matching toothy grins as they stared up at us.

"Trust me, no one has it worse for their man than I do," I informed them truthfully, winking at Landon. The smile I got in response could've lit up an entire city and I was proud that I was able to make him so happy. Landon had brought so much love and joy into my life and I'd sworn to myself that I was going to do everything I could to give it all back to him.

We caught up on what was going on with each other as we ate. Morgan told us about the new community center he'd been asked to build. His business had taken off after the recognition he'd received for building the new Agape House and he deserved every bit of it. He was an amazing man and an excellent contractor.

They asked how things were going with Hamilton Security and I told them about a few of the funnier cases we'd been working. I wish they could all be light-hearted and fun, but unfortunately most of the jobs we took on were of a more serious, and, at times, deadly nature. Only Landon knew some of the darker things my guys and I had to deal with.

I started a pot of coffee, then cut and served the chocolate cake my husband had made for dessert while Akio and Landon talked about their latest project—a band out of the UK that was about to take the world by storm. Lachlan Edwards had recently discovered the band, playing in a pub in England and was so impressed with their sound that he immediately signed them to a contract with his recording studio.

The band was very excited but new to the business. So, Lachlan set them up with Landon as their manager, knowing that they'd be in the best hands possible and wouldn't get taken advantage of. I'd met them when Landon and I took them to dinner one night, and I'd been impressed with the band's leader, Parker Thompson.

He was very good-looking, and I was sure fans would be swooning all over him. But he was also intelligent, kind, and seemed to have a good head on his shoulders. I hoped that didn't change as fame took over, but you never knew how someone would react. I knew Landon would do his best to keep him on the right path though, just as he'd done with Carter and his bandmates.

"I wish you were going to be at my parents' house Christmas Eve like when we were kids," Landon said to Morgan as I sat back down.

"Maybe next year. We're spending this Christmas Eve at Akio's parents' house. My parents are going to be there too," Morgan explained.

"Yeah, it's almost scary how well our parents get along, especially our moms. Don't get me wrong, we're thrilled they've become so close, but it also means they're coming at us as a united front in their efforts to become grandparents. I mean, we just got married," Akio said, exasperation clear in his voice. Landon and I both laughed, but Morgan was wearing a thoughtful expression on his face as he looked at his husband.

"I don't know, maybe they're not wrong," he said quietly. Akio's head swiveled to look at Morgan.

"What?" he asked, his surprise evident.

"I've just been thinking about it and I kind of like the idea of seeing little Akios running around," Morgan said with a shrug.

"Really?" Akio asked, a smile spreading across his face.

I looked over at Landon who was wearing a gentle smile on his own face. I knew what Morgan was talking about because the thought of having a child with Landon, of getting to be fathers together with the man that owned me completely, had been on my mind a lot, even though we'd never really discussed it.

The four of us visited for a while longer before Akio and Morgan left. Landon and I moved around the kitchen quietly as we cleaned up, each of us lost in our own thoughts. I put the last dish in the dishwasher and then turned to find Landon staring at me with a thoughtful look.

"What are you thinking?" I asked as I grabbed the towel off the counter and dried my hands. Landon opened his mouth and then shut it.

"It's nothing," he said with a shrug. I tossed the towel back on the counter and grabbed his arm as he turned to leave, pulling him close and wrapping my arms around his waist.

"Don't do that. I want to know every single thought that goes through that beautiful head of yours," I told him. His eyes softened, and his body melted into mine as he slid his hands around my neck.

"I was just thinking about what Morgan said.

You know, about having a child," Landon whispered. He looked nervous and I wasn't going to have any of that. We'd come too far and been through too much for him to be afraid to say *anything* to me.

"I've been thinking about it too, for a while now," I admitted. He pulled his head back, so he could see me better and I could tell I'd surprised him. "You know how bad things were for me growing up. While I was fortunate to be a part of G's family, and even more blessed when I became a part of your family, I'm a selfish bastard. I want more. I'd like for you and me to create our own family and it doesn't matter to me if we have them biologically or if we adopt, I just want us to be dads."

"I do too. I want everything with you," Landon whispered right before he crushed his mouth to mine. Our kiss held so much love and devotion and a promise for a future that I had never even thought to dream of because I hadn't believed it was possible until I met Landon. Finding him, my soulmate, had opened up an entirely different world for me and I swore that I would cherish every second with him and never take our time together for granted.

As our kiss turned more passionate, a burning need began to build in me and I gripped onto the back of his neck, gently yet forcefully. Landon was shaking as he pulled back to stare into my eyes, but I knew it wasn't from fear or anxiety. The fire burning in his eyes told me that he was feeling the same desire that I was, the same need for more.

"Please," was all he said.

"I want you to go to our room, strip until you're completely bare, and stand at the foot of the bed. You will wait however long it takes until I come to you," I commanded.

Landon visibly trembled, but I saw the small smile playing at his lips as he turned to follow my orders. I smiled as I watched him go. We were perfectly matched in so many ways and we both filled a need within each other. We enjoyed the games we played, and I hoped it never ended.

I grabbed the soap from beneath the sink and filled the dispenser inside the dishwasher then started it. As much as I wanted to race down the hallway and bury myself inside him, I'd take my time and make him wait, letting the anticipation build because there was nothing I loved more than giving my man exactly what he wanted. There would be time to talk about our future and children, but that night was just for the two of us.

CHAPTER
Three

Carter

I NODDED TO ROCKO TO LET HIM KNOW I WAS ready and he raised his drumsticks in the air, tapping them together and counting out 1, 2, 3, 4, before he began a steady beat on the drums in front of him. His closest friends knew him as Rylie, but he liked keeping his personal life separate from his public persona. So, when he was on stage, he was always Rocko. I smiled at him before turning to my other bandmates as the sound of each instrument began to blend together.

Steve was bent over his bass guitar as he played the intro and Tyler followed quickly with his rhythm guitar. His shaggy red hair hung down over one eye, but I saw the wink he gave to his new bride, Kalia, who smiled back at him from her perch over the keyboards. I loved the members of my band and couldn't imagine a better or more talented group of people to work with than them.

Still smiling, I grabbed onto the microphone in front of me. As soon as I sang the first few words from one of our most popular songs, the crowd went wild, and a deafening roar came from all around the sold-out arena. When I reached the chorus, I heard voices chiming in and I closed my eyes and let the sound wash over me. It was a magical thing to hear my own words being sung back to me, one that I would never get tired of.

I opened my eyes and looked down at the swarm of people who were singing and stretching their hands out towards the stage, some of them screaming that they loved me. I appreciated my fans, but there was only one person whose opinion really mattered, only one person whose love I couldn't live without. My husband, Ryan.

I turned my head and saw him standing off to the side of the stage, a lone figure who knew everything there was to know about me; the good, the bad, and the ugly, and still loved me anyway. As usual,

I felt something settle inside me the moment our eyes connected. He smiled at me and a tremor ran through my body.

Ryan was easily the sexiest man I'd ever seen in my life, but it was his spirit, his soul, that had captured my heart. I wasn't sure if it was something his grandfather had instilled in him or if it was just who he was born to be—probably the latter—but Ryan had an innate goodness inside him that was very rare. He had a knack for always finding the bright side in any situation, and he made me want to be a better man.

I played up to the crowd, running around on stage and singing my heart out, but my mind was already back on the bus with Ryan. When he had first started going on tour with me, we had shared a bus with the rest of the band. It had been a tight fit, but we were both so happy to be together that we were willing to sacrifice our comfort.

When it was time to head back out for a second tour, though, I insisted on having our own private bus. Lachlan had readily agreed and had even provided a private bus for Tyler and Kalia as well. Steve and Rylie preferred to share a bus, so they could pass the long hours playing video games with each other. Of course, if Steve's girlfriend was visiting or Lachlan joined Rylie on the tour for a few days, they usually did so when we were playing the same city for several nights and would be able to stay in a hotel.

I finished the last song and was suddenly thrown into darkness as the lights were cut off. My heart was racing, and my body was drenched in sweat as I quickly followed the rest of the band off the stage to the sound of the crowd begging for more. We'd already performed two encores though, so I was satisfied that I'd given them what they needed. What *I* needed was a shower and Ryan, preferably together. He spread his arms as I walked past the curtain, but I held my hands up to stop him.

"I'm a sweaty mess," I explained when he arched a brow at me in question. He gave me a wolfish smile and stepped even closer, disregarding my warning.

"Some of my favorite times are when it's just the two of us, getting all sweaty and messy." Ryan's breath ghosted over my skin as he leaned forward to lick a line up my neck. I shivered against him as he pulled me in and I could feel the evidence of his desire pressing against my leg. "Do you have any idea what those leather pants are doing to me right now?"

"What would it do to you if I took them off?" I asked, lowering my voice seductively. The growl that rumbled from his chest was answer enough and a smile spread across my face. Ryan opened his mouth to respond, but he was interrupted before he got the chance.

"You two need to get a room." I turned to see Rylie walking our way with a broad grin on his face.

"Like you and Lachlan are any better at keeping your hands to yourselves," I teased.

"I just wish he was here," Rylie said with a sigh. "Actually, I wish I was back home with him and our boys."

It was still hard to believe the once extremely wild drummer was a dad. I felt a surge of pride for my friend though. Rylie had been through hell and back, but he'd managed to pull himself up, dust himself off, and make his life better than it had ever been. He'd found his soulmate in Lachlan and the two of them had built a life together which recently had expanded to include two young brothers who looked at their new dads like they hung the moon.

"We just have to get through one more concert and then we can head home, and you can spend Christmas with your family," I told him, giving him a sympathetic smile. I knew how hard it was to be away from the people you loved.

"I can't wait. This Christmas is going to be amazing," Rylie said with an exuberant grin. The joy on his face was evident. "I talked to Lachlan last night and he said that he and Benji got the tree put up, they're just waiting for me to get home, so we can decorate it. The boys helped hang the lights outside and Kerry's been baking up a storm."

"It sounds amazing," I told him.

"Yeah, it does. I just want the boys to have the kind of Christmas I never had growing up. The kind I'm sure they never got to have either. They're great kids and they deserve to feel safe and happy and loved. They deserve the chance to be kids," Rylie said with a faraway look in his eyes.

I could tell that his thoughts were back in Chicago and I grabbed Ryan's hand, giving it a gentle squeeze. I was so thankful to have him with me all the time. Being apart from one another for months at a time had been very difficult for both of us and we'd promised to never go that long again without seeing each other. The look he gave me told me that he was thinking the same thing.

"Anyway, I'm going to get a shower and call home. You guys have a good night," Rylie said, smiling once again. I watched him walk off then turned back to my husband.

"Where were we?" I asked, waggling my brows at him as I slid my arms up over his shoulders.

He gazed down at me with a sexy, sultry look in his eyes and my cock twitched in response. This man could turn me inside out with just a simple look or word. Most of the time, all he had to do was walk in the room and I was ready to rip his clothes off and devour him whole. I didn't have a clue what I'd ever done to deserve a man like him, but I was going to enjoy the hell out of every single second of our lives together.

"I was getting ready to take you to our bus and peel you out of those clothes, so I could lick the sweat off your body," he said, his voice coming out husky and strained. I was thankful that no one was around to hear the embarrassingly loud groan that escaped me. My cock was rock hard and pressing uncomfortably against the zipper of my pants.

"Yeah, let's do that." I nodded my head enthusiastically. In my lust-driven rush to get to the bus and start the fun, it took me several moments to realize that Ryan wasn't beside me. I turned around and found him strolling a few feet behind. I waited for him to catch up. "You okay?" I asked him.

"I'm great. Just enjoying the view," he said with a leer as he looked at my ass. "I like the way that tight, black leather accentuates your perfectly curved ass."

I swallowed hard. I could feel my cock leaking

inside my pants. We had reached a more crowded area behind the stage where the crew was working hard to dismantle the stage and pack everything up so we could move on to the next city. We needed to get out of there soon if I didn't want to find a picture of me and my husband in a compromising position, splashed all over the front page of tomorrow's news. Not that I thought any of the crew would do that. They'd seen us together plenty of times and had always been considerate of our privacy, but you never knew when a paparazzi might be lurking, and I'd learned long ago to take precautions.

I grabbed Ryan's hand and pulled him along with me as I wove through the throng of people and made my way to the exit. I smiled at the security guard that stood there and we waited as he opened the door and checked the area before leading us outside. Another guard was standing outside our bus and assured us that no one had gotten inside.

The security measures that Micah had outlined for the men he'd sent to watch over the members of the band may have seemed a little over the top, but I knew that he had his reasons for wanting to keep us safe and they went beyond his love for my brother. Ryan and I were his family and it warmed my heart that he took such care with us.

I climbed the steps into the bus and closed my eyes as I took a deep breath and slowly released it. After the rumbling noise of the concert, the silence of the bus was a welcome reprieve and I felt the tension ebb from my body.

I loved the rush of performing in front of thousands of fans, but nothing compared to time alone with Ryan in our own space. The bus was our sanctuary, as close to home as we could get. It was the one place on the road where Ryan and I could shut out the rest of the world and just be ourselves.

The sound of the lock clicking into place had me opening my eyes and I turned to face the man I loved. His eyes were dark and hooded as he looked me up and down and when his gaze locked with mine, I slowly licked my lips in invitation.

We stepped forward at the same time, closing the distance between us. Our mouths crashed together, teeth clacking and tongues searching, as our hands began to explore; as if we'd been apart for weeks instead of hours. Shirts were ripped and tossed aside as we fumbled our way down the narrow hall to our bedroom.

"Please, Ryan," I begged in between kisses. I didn't even try to hide my neediness for him. Ryan knew me better than anyone, so it would be pointless.

He gently lowered me to the bed and hovered over me, his blue-gray eyes serious as he stared at me.

"All those people, millions of fans around the world who listen to your music, they know your name and they see your face everywhere. They pay money to see you perform and they dream of meeting you, wishing they could spend even just a few minutes with you. But somehow, for some reason, you chose me." His words were said in awe, but I felt the need to reassure him anyway. I placed my hands on either side of his face and leaned up, gently kissing his eyelids, the tip of his nose, and over both cheeks, before pulling back to look at him.

"You are my best friend, the love of my life, and my soulmate. None of that other stuff matters if I don't have you by my side. You are the kindest, bravest, most incredible man I've ever known, and I will never want anyone but you," I told him.

"I know you don't want anyone else. I trust you and I trust what we have together. Sometimes it just all seems unreal when I'm watching you out on stage," Ryan admitted quietly. I knew he didn't doubt my love for him, but it also couldn't be easy to have to share me with thousands of strangers night after night. I wasn't sure I would have been able to handle it as well as he had if our roles were reversed, so if my man needed some reassurance once in a while, I was more than happy to oblige.

"Do I need to convince you how very real this is?" I asked as I lifted my hips. Ryan sucked in a breath as our covered cocks rubbed against each other and he bent his head, sealing his lips over mine in a passionate kiss that, once again, stoked the flames within us.

"I might need a little more convincing," he teased, and I was glad to see the clouds gone from his eyes, replaced with a burning desire.

I reached down and unbuttoned his jeans, letting my finger dip inside to graze over the tip of his cock. It was slick and wet, and I pulled my finger out and sucked it into my mouth, moaning at the taste of his salty, sweet fluid.

"Fuck, that's hot," Ryan growled then he jumped from the bed and quickly finished undressing.

"No, *that's* fucking hot," I said, my mouth watering at the sight of his long dick. I knew every ridge and vein of that cock, but I never got tired of seeing it, tasting it, feeling it inside me. He grabbed a bottle of lube from the drawer and then moved to the foot of the bed.

"I seemed to remember something about licking the sweat from your body," he said.

"I'm all yours," I told him. I folded my hands under my head and grinned up at him.

"Yes, you are," he said firmly as he knelt on the bed. I was relieved to hear the confidence back in his voice.

Ryan climbed up my body, his legs on either side of me and unbuttoned my pants. I breathed a sigh of relief as he unzipped them and then pulled them down past my hips. My cock sprang out and landed on my stomach with a soft slap, leaving a sticky trail behind that glistened in the soft lighting of our room. He bent down and licked it before tugging my pants off the rest of the way.

True to his word, Ryan continued lapping at my naked flesh with his tongue until I thought I would lose my mind. His teeth grazed over my nipple and he bit down, sucking it into his mouth. My fingers dove into his hair and I held his head in place as he pleasured me.

"Ryan! I need you," I pleaded. He lifted his head to look at me and slid up so that we were face-to-face.

"What is it you need? Tell me," he commanded.

"I need your cock inside me," I begged.

He nodded his head once and then sat up and reached for the lube. He slicked himself quickly and then kissed me as he worked his fingers inside me, preparing my body to accept him. I lifted my knees, but was surprised when he dropped down beside me on the bed.

"I want you to ride me. Use my body for your own pleasure and show me how much you love me," he whispered in my ear and I gasped at the eroticism of his words.

I sat up and threw my leg over him, so I was straddling his hips then I looked into his eyes as I reached behind me and grasped his cock in my hand. I rubbed up and down it a few times, watching as his eyes rolled back in his head and his tongue darted out to wet his lips. With his miles of flawless, golden skin and rippling abs, my man was breathtaking.

I lifted up on my knees and lined the head of his cock up with my entrance and then I began to slide down his length. His hands went to my waist where he held me securely as I lowered myself even further. Ryan was big, but my body knew his and welcomed him inside easily.

When I had taken him in all the way, I sat there, my fingers smoothing over his chest and reveling in the feeling of fullness and completeness that I had only ever felt when I was with him. It went beyond two bodies coming together. What Ryan and I had was almost spiritual, a merging of two souls.

I bent down to kiss him and then I began to move. I showed him with my movements and my touch and the words that were whispered between us that he was the only man for me, the only man I would ever love. And when we lay gasping for air, each of us spent and sated, there was no doubt at all that what we had was real.

CHAPTER
Four

Akio

I MADE A FEW NOTES IN MY TABLET AS LANDON listed the last-minute things that needed to be done before our newest clients could head out on tour. Landon was one of the best entertainment managers in the business and he'd quickly secured their spot as the opening act for a very popular band. If everything went as expected, they would be headlining their own tour within the next year. I double-checked that everything had been added to my schedule and then shut my tablet, turning to Landon with a smile.

"Are you sure you don't want me to help you

with all of this?" Landon asked.

"Nah, it won't take me more than a couple of hours. Morgan's working tomorrow anyway so I can finish this up in the morning and still have time to wrap his presents before he gets home. You've been working so hard lately, you deserve to spend time with your family," I insisted.

"Thanks, I really appreciate that. Christmas has always been my favorite holiday, but this one is going to be extra special. Our family has grown so much. We all have someone special to celebrate with and we also have my nieces and nephew," he explained.

I could see the excitement in my best friend's eyes as he talked about the presents he and Micah had bought the kids and my mind drifted to Morgan's comment from the night before about wanting children. I wasn't opposed to the idea at all, but I'd been surprised because we hadn't really talked about it before. After all, we'd only been married a couple of months, but Morgan brought it up again on the drive home and I could tell that he'd put a lot of thought into it already.

I sat in the cab of his truck, warmed by both the heater and his words, as he described all the things he wanted to do with our future children. It was probably silly, given the fact that we were married and fully committed to each other, but hearing him speak about starting a family together made it seem that much more real to me. I was still amazed that a man as wonderful as Morgan wanted to spend the rest of his life with me. Now, it seemed like all I could think about was Morgan holding a baby.

"What?" I asked when I realized Landon had asked me a question. He chuckled at me, knowing my mind had wandered.

"I asked if you were going to get together with your friends from college over the holidays," he repeated.

"Oh, yeah. Jasper invited us over for a New Year's Eve party. We'll probably stop in for a little while," I told him.

"Is everything okay between you guys?" Landon asked, giving me a concerned look.

"Yeah. I feel guilty not telling them the truth about why Garrett took off. I know they've been worried about him, we all have. But I've done enough damage to Garrett. The least I can do is keep quiet about what happened. If he wants them to know, he can tell them himself. That is, if he ever calls," I said.

"You still haven't heard from him?" Landon asked gently.

Landon was my best friend, so I'd confided in

him about everything that had happened. It had come as a complete surprise to me that my old friend had developed feelings for me, but by the time I'd found out, I'd already fallen completely head over heels for Morgan. Things had gotten pretty ugly the night Garrett finally made his move and ended up on the other side of Morgan's fist. Morgan had proven once again what an amazing man he was when, despite being pissed at Garrett, he had arranged for the two of us to meet so we could talk things through. Garrett had said that he didn't blame me for any of what had happened, but he'd still ended up leaving, saying he needed time to heal. Time away from me.

"He texted to say that he was safe, but that was all. I have no idea where he is or how long he'll be gone. He's always considered me, Jasper, and Travis his family. We're all he's got and now he's out there, all alone over the holidays and it's my fault," I said miserably.

"None of what happened is your fault," Landon said, grabbing my hand and holding it in between his.

"But I should've seen that he was developing feelings for me," I insisted. "Maybe if I'd noticed what was going on, I could've talked to him about it before things got so out of hand."

"Look, I get that Garrett's upset and he needs some time away to get his head on straight, but none of this is your fault. I'm sure he had his reasons, but he kept his feelings a secret for a long time and that was *his* choice. You shouldn't blame yourself for not seeing something he didn't want you to see. Do you believe in soulmates?" Landon asked.

"Of course, Morgan is my soulmate," I answered, confused by the sudden change in subject.

"I do too," he said with a smile. "If you believe that, then you have to believe that Garrett will find his when it's time. Just give him some time, he'll come around eventually. And remember, if Garrett gets lonely over the holidays, he knows where to find you guys. It's his decision." Landon gave me a pointed look and I nodded my understanding.

"You're right, I just hope Garrett comes home soon. I miss my friend," I told him with a shrug.

"I know you do," Landon said gently, giving my hand a squeeze. "Hey, Micah and I were going to get some dinner with Caleb and Giovanni and then go out to the tree farm and cut down a Christmas tree to take to Agape House. Why don't you and Morgan come with us? It'll cheer you up," Landon suggested.

"Are you sure?" I asked.

"You're my best friend and you're married to my

favorite cousin. Of course I want to spend time with you guys," he responded cheerfully.

"Okay, I'll call Morgan," I told him. He stood up and started collecting the files we had spread out in front of us. I grabbed his arm to get his attention before making the call. "Thanks, Landon," I said sincerely. He bent down and wrapped his arms around me.

"Anytime. It'll all work out, trust me," he whispered. I hugged him back, swallowing around the lump in my throat. After a few seconds, he moved away, and I picked up my phone. Landon was right, Garrett was an adult and he'd come home when he was ready. It was time to focus on my husband and our first Christmas together.

"Hey, baby!" Morgan said an hour later as he slid into the booth next to me. His lips brushed over mine and I closed my eyes and breathed in his scent, letting his familiar smell wash away the last of my sadness. I was smiling when I pulled back and he answered with a smile of his own.

"Hey there," I whispered.

"Okay, you two, that's enough. No making out over the food," Caleb teased, and everyone laughed.

We had a great time at dinner as we all shared pizza and swapped funny stories from our

Christmases past. Giovanni, Micah, and I were laughing so hard we had tears in our eyes as Caleb, Morgan, and Landon described some of the antics they'd gotten up to as kids.

"Remember Carter's Holiday talent show?" Landon said with a chuckle.

"You mean, the *Extravaganza*?" Caleb said with a flourish.

"Oh, yes! The Holiday *Extravaganza*! I'll never forget it," Morgan clarified with a laugh. "Even as a kid, Carter wanted to be the center of attention, so he was always putting on these talent shows and gathering the whole family around to watch," he explained to us.

"Carter had been practicing his act for weeks and he was really excited about it. He went all out with costumes and even had Emma and Michelle in on the act as his backup dancers," Landon added.

"He wanted a big audience, so he decided to do it when the entire family was together for Christmas Eve. We were at our grandparents' house, as well as all of our aunts, uncles, and cousins," Morgan continued. "So, Carter strutted out with his jeans down off his hips and his underwear hanging out and he starts belting out some song into a microphone." Morgan choked on a laugh and I laughed with him because his laughter was contagious.

"Only it turns out it wasn't a microphone at all," Landon said around his laughter.

"What was it?" Giovanni asked.

"Grandma's vibrator," Caleb answered. Our table roared with laughter, causing more than a few curious glances to be sent our way, but we were all beyond the point of caring.

"I'd never seen Dad move that fast as he wrestled it out of Carter's hands and ran from the room," Landon sputtered.

"How old was he?" Micah asked.

"We were ten," Caleb told him.

"Oh my God! That's hysterical. What did your grandparents say?" I asked.

"Grandpa told Grandma she needed to find a better hiding place for their toys," Morgan said with a shrug.

"Well, I guess the apple doesn't fall far from the tree," Micah murmured. Landon gave him a questioning look. "That has to be where your parents get it from. They're not exactly shy about the fun they get up to with each other."

"That's true," Landon agreed, chuckling again.

"Oh man, do you think we'll be that bad with our kids?" Caleb said in mock horror.

"We can only hope," Giovanni teased. "Besides, I'm not so sure it's a bad thing. Your parents and grandparents may have shocked you a time or two with their behavior, but I bet you never had to question how they truly felt about each other."

Everyone nodded their heads in agreement and Morgan slid his arm around me, pulling me closer so he could whisper in my ear. His warm breath blowing across my neck made me shiver and my cock began to respond as he spoke.

"I can't wait to have kids that we can embarrass. Our children will know every single day how much I love their father," he said. Warmth spread throughout my chest as I turned my head to gaze at him adoringly. Everything I could ever want was right there in front of me. Any children we had in the future would just be the icing on an already perfect cake.

"I can't wait for that either. I love you," I whispered.

Morgan's hand slid to the back of my neck and he pulled me in for a kiss, his lips gently pressing against mine. The sound of someone clearing their throat had me pulling back and I felt my face heat up when I was met with the knowing smirks of the two other couples.

"Come on, we better get out of here before we get kicked out because the newlyweds can't keep their hands off each other," Landon joked.

Morgan flipped him the bird and we all laughed as we tossed some money on the table and filed out of the restaurant. It was just beginning to snow as we stepped outside into the brisk winter air. Big fluffy flakes fell down all around us, coating the ground and we all took a minute to soak in the beauty.

It didn't take long for us to drive to the Christmas tree farm where Morgan climbed out of the truck and made his way around to open my door. I smiled at the gesture and he winked at me as he offered his hand to help me down from the cab of the truck. As soon as my feet hit the ground, I stood on my toes to place a kiss on his lips, showing him my appreciation.

"What was that for?" he asked with a smile as he wrapped my scarf around my neck.

"For being you," I replied, and his eyes softened as he grinned at me.

Morgan slid on a pair of gloves and grabbed a saw and tape measure from the back of his truck before we walked over to where our friends were waiting. I trailed behind my husband as we made our way through the rows of evergreens, enjoying the delectable view of his ass encased in his jeans.

"So, how tall are the ceilings at Agape House? I want to get the biggest tree we can for the kids," Giovanni said.

"Trust me, the ceilings are taller than any tree out here," Morgan assured him. "Feel free to get the biggest and best one you can find."

Giovanni and Micah paused to give each other a look and then let out a loud victory cry before taking off running towards the back field where the largest trees stood. The rest of us followed along, laughing at their boyish excitement.

"When are Ryan and Carter supposed to get home?" I asked Caleb. The two of us had decided to hang back while the others argued over whether to get a full tree or one where the branches were more spaced apart.

"Tomorrow," he answered, his face lighting up with his smile.

"I bet you're excited to see them." I grinned back.

"You have no idea," Caleb responded with a sigh. "It's hard to explain to people who don't have a twin, but things just always feel a little off when Carter and I are apart. Almost like I'm missing an arm or something. I'm so happy for him that he gets to go on tour and do what he loves, but I can't wait to have him back here."

"I'm sure it's hard for him to be away from you too. It's good that you have each other. I always wished I'd had siblings," I said wistfully.

"Well, we may not be siblings, but you've got all of us and we're family now," Caleb said sweetly, threading his arm through mine. Morgan turned just then with his eyes sparkling with happiness and big flakes of snow falling down all around him and I felt a moment of complete rightness, like I was exactly where I was supposed to be.

"I love you," he mouthed, and my heart fluttered inside my chest.

The guys finally agreed on a tree and Micah went to work cutting it down. When he was finished, Giovanni and Landon drug it onto a sled that the farm had provided and began hauling it back toward the parking lot. We took turns quoting some of our favorite Christmas movies as we went, including National Lampoon's Christmas Vacation. We were still laughing as we got in line to pay and I had to admit that Landon had been right. Going out with my friends had been exactly what I needed to get my mind off my troubles and put me in the spirit of Christmas.

"Guys, I just had a fantastic idea," Landon said slowly, turning to us with a devious smile. I wasn't sure what he had in mind, but whatever it was, he could count me in.

CHAPTER
Five

Rylie

"HOLY SHIT! THIS IS ONE FANCY PLANE," Tyler said.

"That's because it's a private jet," Kalia informed him.

Tyler let out a whistle as he looked around at the lush leather seats, the enormous TV mounted to the front wall and the fully stocked bar in the corner. I laughed quietly. I'd long since gotten used to my husband's extravagant tastes. Lachlan Edwards didn't do anything halfway, whether it was buying a company jet, running his music empire or his latest project, opening a nightclub.

The only thing he put more time and effort into was loving me and our little family. Despite all his fortune and success, nothing mattered more to Lachlan than me and the boys and he made it clear to everyone that worked for him that the three of us were his top priority.

And that was how the band and I ended up flying home on a private jet in the middle of a snowstorm when most planes were being delayed. Lachlan wanted me home almost as much as I wanted to get home, and he would stop at nothing to make that happen.

"Man, I can't wait to get home," my best friend, Steve, said. "My mom made her famous peanut butter fudge and she saved a plate, just for me."

"I'm looking forward to sleeping in our own bed," Kalia said and Tyler pulled her towards him, whispering something in her ear that made her face flame red.

"I second that," Ryan added, waggling his eyes at Carter who leaned over and gave him a kiss.

"I can't wait to see our family. I bet our nieces and nephew have grown a lot while we've been gone. I couldn't believe how much they'd changed when we saw them at Thanksgiving," Carter said to his husband.

"You need some time with Caleb too," Ryan said

knowingly. A look of longing came over Carter's face and I could see his eyes turn glassy as he nodded.

"We better sleep on the way home so we're not too tired once we get there," Kalia suggested as the jet took off.

We all voiced our agreement and I smiled at my friends as we settled into our seats for the long flight home. It had been a whirlwind tour, starting in the States then moving onto Asia before winding down in Europe. It was an amazing experience and we were thrilled that every show had been sold out, but I think we were all ready to get back home. We'd been going almost nonstop for over a year and we deserved a break.

"Is there anything I can get for you, Mr. Edwards?" the flight attendant asked me. I smiled at the sound of my married name. I didn't get to hear it often since most of the world still knew me as Rocko instead of Rylie Edwards, but those who worked for Lachlan had signed an NDA so that I could be myself around them.

"No, thank you, Iris. I think we're just going to sleep most of the way."

"Of course, sir. Just press the button on your chair if you need anything at all," she answered pleasantly.

She returned a minute later with a stack of neatly folded blankets and passed them out to everyone then turned the lights off. I reclined my seat and snuggled down into the warm blanket, the hectic schedule and lack of sleep finally catching up to me. I was surrounded by the soft snores and gentle whispers of my friends, but my mind was already back home with my husband and two boys as I drifted off to sleep.

Hours later, after dropping off each of my friends at their houses, the limo finally pulled into the driveway of the home I shared with Lachlan. An excited fluttering started in my stomach at the thought of seeing him again, holding him, kissing him. It was still dark out, the barest hint of light beginning to show over the horizon and I knew everyone would probably be asleep. In fact, I was counting on it.

It was quiet as I crept inside and up the dark staircase. I paused by the boys' room and carefully opened their door, peeking my head inside. My heart felt like it was going to burst when I saw them cuddled together, sound asleep, their sweet faces lit up by the nightlight plugged into the wall.

Eventually we hoped they'd feel comfortable enough to have rooms of their own, but they'd only been with us a few weeks and we knew it would take some time. Given the horrors that had been dealt them at the hands of their own mother, if they felt safer sharing a room, then that's exactly what they'd do.

I closed the door and made my way down the long hallway to the last bedroom on the right and slipped inside, locking the door behind me. By then, the first light of day was beginning to creep in through the window and I was able to make out Lachlan's sleeping form on the bed. I moved quietly as I discarded my clothes and lifted the blankets, so I could crawl between the sheets.

Lachlan stirred as I slid in behind him and wrapped my arm around his waist, pulling him close. My lips ghosted over the smooth skin at the back of his neck and I drew in a deep breath, filling my lungs with the familiar sleep-warmed scent of my husband. This, to me, was home. Not the city or the mansion, but the man in my arms. Lachlan was everything I could've hoped for and nothing I deserved, but by some miracle, he'd chosen me to share his life with.

"Rylie," he whispered in the dark and that was all it took for me to grow fully hard, my cock beginning to leak at the sound of his voice.

"I'm home, baby," I answered, and he turned in my arms.

His smile stole my breath away and I tilted my head and covered his mouth with my own. My tongue teased along the seam of his lips until he granted me entry and I moaned at the first taste of him. I scooted towards him, but it wasn't close enough. I needed to feel his skin against mine, his heart pounding against my chest as I held him in my arms. I needed to re-connect with him and to erase the many miles that had been put between us over the last several weeks.

I reached for the hem of his t-shirt and tugged on it. Lachlan must have sensed my urgency because he pulled back long enough to rip the shirt over his head and toss it to the floor. I helped him shimmy out of his sleep pants next, throwing them over my shoulder then I rolled on top of him.

Lachlan spread his legs, so I could settle myself between them and we both moaned as our cocks rubbed together. I rested my forearms on either side of him and leaned my forehead against his. My long hair hung down around our faces, acting as a curtain to shield us from the rest of the world.

"I missed you so damn much," I whispered.

"I missed you too. I'm glad you're home," he responded then he bit down on my bottom lip, tugging it gently between his teeth and scrambling my brain.

I pressed my lips to his and then sat up,

straddling him so I could see him better. My eyes moved hungrily over the smooth plane of his chest, down over his flat stomach, to the thin line of hair that disappeared underneath where I was sitting. Lachlan stared up at me and the look in his eyes told me everything I needed to know; I was wanted, I was cherished, I was loved. I swallowed around the lump in my throat as my emotions threatened to overwhelm me.

We reached for each other at the same time, our hands trailing over the other's body; exploring, memorizing, rediscovering. I shifted so I could grasp our cocks together and felt a surge of pride when Lachlan's eyes rolled to the back of his head as I began to jerk my fist up and down.

"Please, Rylie," he gasped.

"Please, what?" I teased.

"Please, put your cock inside me," he said through clenched teeth. I bent down and licked the shell of his ear.

"I know, I just wanted to hear you say it out loud. It makes me so hard," I whispered, and I felt his body tremble beneath me.

With that, I reached into the drawer beside the bed and pulled out a bottle of lube then I moved so I was kneeling between his legs. I coated my fingers quickly and then reached out, running a wet finger over his balls and down to his tight little hole. Lachlan lifted his hips, eagerly searching for more as I circled his rim. Finally, I slid a finger in and began to slowly and carefully open him up.

I added more fingers and Lachlan kept up a steady stream of dirty talk which, delivered in his sexy British accent, had me hard as a rock and right on the edge in only a matter of seconds. After a month of nothing but phone sex and naked Skyping, I'd be damned if I was going to come before I got inside him though. I removed my fingers and stared at him through hooded eyes as I reached for the bottle of lube and poured a line over my cock, working it over my shaft with my palm.

"Are you ready?" My voice was deep and husky when I spoke, and Lachlan raised his knees to his chest, exposing himself to me in answer.

I fisted my cock and lined the head up with his entrance, then I slowly pressed forward, watching as my dick disappeared inside his tight heat. I held still, giving him time to adjust, but Lachlan wasn't interested in waiting. He circled his legs around my waist and dug his heels into my ass, urging me forward until I was buried balls deep inside him.

I bent down, and we shared a passionate kiss

as his hands slid around my neck and into my hair, gripping me as if he were afraid I'd disappear. I had no intention of going anywhere, though. I was exactly where I wanted to be. I began to rock my hips, gently at first and then with more purposeful strokes. Lachlan writhed underneath me, moaning and chanting my name as I pegged his prostate with an accuracy that came with knowing his body almost better than I knew my own.

His cock leaked between us, coating both our stomachs in sticky fluid. His hand reached between us and he began jerking his dick, using rapid movements as he raced toward his orgasm. I kept up a steady pace as I clenched my jaw, fighting to hold onto my last thread of control as my balls drew up tightly to my body and threatened to erupt.

I managed to stave off my orgasm until I felt Lachlan arch up off the bed, his head pressing into the pillow and the veins in his neck straining as his own release rushed through him. He let out a guttural cry as his seed splashed between us, hot and wet. He was totally uninhibited in that moment, a slave to his base desires, and he was magnificent.

The sight of my husband coming undone was enough to send white heat racing through my veins and I thrust into him once more before spilling my seed inside him. I was shaking as the last surges of my orgasm began to ebb and I collapsed on top of him, completely sated and deliriously happy. Lachlan's arms came around me and I felt his lips in my hair as he kissed me. I lifted my head and pushed my lips out in offering. A warm smile lifted his lips as he bent his head to kiss me.

"I love you. Welcome home," he whispered.

"I love you too, Lachlan," I said with a smile.

After a few minutes, things began to get uncomfortable and I carefully slid out of him and flopped down on the bed next to him with a sigh. The room was lit up with the morning's rays and I watched in confusion when Lachlan climbed from the bed, holding a hand out to me.

"We don't have much time before the boys will be up and they probably shouldn't see us like this," he explained, gesturing to the cum that glistened in his navel. I laughed as understanding dawned.

"Yeah, you're probably right," I conceded, taking his hand. Lachlan glanced at the clock next to the bed and then waggled his eyebrows at me.

"If we hurry, we might have time for some shower fun though," he said, already walking away. He looked over his shoulder and let out a laugh as I jumped up from the bed and raced after him.

We ended up spending more time in the shower than was appropriate and by the time we made it downstairs, we could hear the boys talking to Kerry in the kitchen as she cooked their breakfast. I'd talked to the boys every day while I was away, either through phone calls, Skype or texting. I wanted to get to know them better and I wanted them to know me and it seemed to have worked.

Still, I worried that they would feel like I was a stranger once I came home. As we neared the kitchen, I steeled myself for whatever their reaction might be. I loved them and if it took them some time to warm up to me or trust me, then I would put the time and effort into making that happen.

Lachlan must have sensed my nervousness because he reached down and grabbed my hand, giving it a gentle squeeze before pushing the door open. Four sets of eyes turned to us and I swallowed thickly. Kerry was the first to respond and she ran toward me and grabbed me in a tight hug as Benjamin placed a plate of pancakes on the table.

"I'm so glad you're home. This place just isn't the same without you," she said sweetly, and I felt tears pool in my eyes as I hugged her back and breathed in her familiar smell. Kerry was so much more than a cook and a housekeeper, she was family and the closest thing I'd ever had to a mother.

"I'm glad to be home," I whispered. She patted my cheek and gave me a knowing look before bustling back over to finish cooking.

I turned to the boys then who were both seated at the table. Dylan, the older of the two, looked more curious than skeptical as he watched me, his hair falling over into his bright green eyes. He'd gained some weight since I'd been away, making him look less gaunt and giving him a healthy glow. He was a handsome boy and I pitied all the poor boys who would try to gain his attention. Eight-year-old Max grinned up at me, obviously not shy at all and I grinned back. He didn't move from his seat however, and I lowered myself into a chair, so I wasn't looming over him. My eyes darted back and forth between the two, soaking them in while I tried to figure out what to say.

"How long are you here for?" Dylan spoke up, breaking the awkward silence before I could. I looked at Lachlan first and he gave me a supportive smile. I cleared my throat and then turned back to Dylan.

"We decided to take an extended break. We'll keep recording albums, but we won't be touring for at least a couple of years," I told him. I could hear the blood rushing through my ears over the silence in the room and then I saw the most beautiful grin spread across my son's face.

"Cool," he said nonchalantly and then he grabbed a pancake from the top of the stack and began smothering it in syrup. Seeing his brother's easy acceptance, Max jumped out of his seat and climbed onto my lap. His jet-black hair and crystal-blue eyes shone as he smiled up at me.

"We waited to put the decorations on the tree and Benjamin said we couldn't make the cookies yet," he informed me.

"Why is that?" I asked, feeling completely charmed by his dimples.

"He said we couldn't do those things until the whole family was here and you're family, silly," he said as if it were the most obvious thing in the world. My head shot up and I looked directly at the older man who was looking down at the towel in his hands as if it were the most interesting thing in the world.

"Did you say that, Benji?" I asked.

"I do not recall my exact words," he said with a huff, tossing the towel onto the counter and taking a seat with the rest of us at the table. Max scooted off my lap and began to eat as the rest of us passed plates of food around. We all dug in and I caught Benjamin's eye as Max started to name all the things he had put on his list for Santa.

"Thank you," I mouthed. Benjamin gave me a subtle wink and then turned to Dylan, asking what he wanted for Christmas.

I felt Lachlan's hand on my leg and I reached down, linking our fingers together as I looked around the table with a huge smile on my face and a heart that was full. It was definitely good to be home.

CHAPTER
Six

Carter

I T WAS STILL DARK OUT WHEN WE GOT HOME, the sun having yet to make its appearance for the day. Ryan and I had already decided to forgo any unpacking, choosing to head straight to bed instead and get a little more sleep before we had to be at my parents' house for lunch. We'd slept as much as possible on the flight home, but it was hard to sleep well when we were in recliners instead of a bed and had the sound of Steve's snoring to wake us up every few minutes. We dropped our bags by the front door and I let out a weary sigh, thankful to be home.

"Come on, baby. Let's go to bed," Ryan said,

taking my hand in his and leading me past the pool table and arcade games we had on the lower level of our home and to the stairs that led up to the living area. Ryan had converted his grandfather's old textile warehouse into a home before I met him and since I'd moved in, we'd made some alterations to make it both of ours.

There was now a collection of framed gold and platinum albums hanging on the walls in the game room as well as various awards I'd received for my music. The open-floor living space upstairs held framed photos of the two of us and our family members on every available flat surface. A keyboard and my favorite guitar were in the corner of the living room along with stacks of papers that held the notes of songs I'd written in various stages of completion.

I told Ryan that we should build a soundproof room downstairs, so I wouldn't disturb him while I worked, but he insisted that he liked being there, watching me as I composed a new song. I had to admit, I preferred having him near too. Not only did he serve as inspiration for my songs, but having him close always settled some restless part inside of me.

I followed behind him as we made our way upstairs, taking a moment to admire the way Ryan's jeans hugged his ass. Despite how tired I was, I could feel my cock responding to the way his thighs bunched beneath the denim as he climbed the stairs. *Maybe we could muster up enough energy for a quickie before we both fall asleep.* I was just getting ready to suggest that when he stopped suddenly at the top of the stairs.

"What the hell?" he exclaimed.

"What's wrong?" I gave him a little nudge and he stepped aside so I could move to stand next to him and my jaw dropped when I saw the condition of our living room.

Bright, colorful streamers were hung from the middle of the ceiling and draped outward in a tent-like display, and there were helium balloons hanging everywhere in a variety of shapes and sizes. As my eyes traveled around the room, I noticed several unicorns, rainbows, and at least one balloon shaped like a man in a speedo. That wasn't the end of it though.

Standing in the middle of the room was the brightest, gaudiest tree I'd ever seen. In fact, it looked more like a Pride float than a Christmas tree. It was lit up with what appeared to be penis-shaped lights and as I stepped closer, I saw it was decorated in every sex toy imaginable. There were cock rings and butt plugs, cock cages and bottles of lube hanging on every single branch. Anal beads were strung throughout the pine needles like garland and perched on the very top, in place of an angel, was a golden Fleshlight.

We stared silently for several minutes as we took it all in and then we both started to laugh; a small chuckle at first and then growing until we were doubled over and had tears running down our cheeks. When we were finally able to catch our breath, Ryan reached for the card that was placed strategically in the center of the branches.

"Welcome home. Let the games begin," he read aloud then turned to me with a questioning look.

"This has my brothers written all over it," I stated, looking around to admire their handiwork once again.

"I figured as much," Ryan said drolly. "Go on."

"Well, as you know, my siblings and I can get a bit competitive," I began, laughing at the way Ryan arched his brow at me. He knew all too well our competitive nature.

"When we were kids and were off school for winter break, we'd keep ourselves busy and out of Mom's hair by creating little competitions. Anything from who could string the most popcorn in under a minute, to who could fit the most Christmas cookies in their mouth at once. I won that last one, by the way," I added, smiling proudly.

"Yeah, you did," Ryan said, giving me a saucy wink.

"Anyway, as we got older, the competitions became a tradition of sorts. We missed one year when Caleb was in Europe. It just didn't feel right to do it without him. I wondered if they would want to pick it back up now that everyone will be together this year, but no one had said anything, so I wasn't sure," I said with a shrug. Ryan walked over to me and wrapped his arms around my waist. My hands automatically lifted to his hair, running my fingers through his silky strands.

"It looks like the tradition is going to continue and you have an even better chance of winning now," Ryan said as his hands moved south of my waist and cupped my ass, kneading it.

"Oh, yeah? Why is that?" I asked, smiling up at him.

"Because you have me as a partner," he stated. I gasped as he suddenly lifted me up in the air and I clung to him, my legs circling his waist as he carried me over to our bed.

"We *are* an unstoppable team," I told him as I laid kisses all over his face. Ryan murmured his agreement then captured my mouth with his in a tantalizing kiss.

"I think we need to have our own little welcome home party before we go to sleep," he said, and I let out a laugh as he dropped me onto the bed.

My laughter soon died however as I took in the molten look in his eyes and I nearly swallowed my tongue as he pulled a set of anal beads out of his pocket. *When had he managed to swipe those off the tree without me noticing?* Desire blew through me like a raging fire and I wondered how my body hadn't turned to ash already. We hurried to strip ourselves out of our clothes and then Ryan proceeded to pleasure me until I'd lost track of how many orgasms we'd each had and we both drifted off into a blissful slumber.

Several hours later, we were showered and dressed and feeling a lot more rested as we drove to my parents' house. A thick blanket of snow was on the ground and still hadn't slowed its descent from the sky as it drifted down in big, beautiful flakes, turning the city of Chicago into a winter wonderland. The weatherman had predicted that we would continue to get snow over the next few days, ensuring that we'd be able to enjoy a white Christmas.

We left the city behind and drove through the suburbs until we reached the more rural area where my parents lived. I smiled as we passed familiar houses and the school where my siblings and I had all gone as kids. I'd been all over the world and met thousands of people along the way, but there was just nothing like coming home, back to the people who knew who I really was and loved me just for being me.

By the look of all the vehicles in the driveway when we pulled in, we were the last to arrive and we jumped from the car, each of us excited to get inside and see everyone. Ryan met me at the front of the car and we held hands as we walked up the sidewalk and onto the porch.

We were greeted with the sounds of many voices talking all at once and peals of laughter that I knew belonged to my sisters. Ryan held out his hand and I gave him my coat to hang up as I kicked off my snow-covered shoes. I closed my eyes and took a deep breath as I waited for Ryan to get his shoes off.

I'd heard before that the sense of smell was our strongest sense and that it could stir memories faster than any of our other senses. I believed that was true because every time I stepped into my parents' house, I was flooded with memories. It didn't matter that my parents had repainted or installed new carpeting throughout the house. These smells had imbedded themselves into the walls, as if the house wanted to hold onto all the love and laughter and good times that had been shared by the family that had lived there.

I opened my eyes, brushing off my sentimental musings. I didn't need to cling to thoughts of my family as I had done on the road—they were there, in the flesh and just on the other side of that door. All conversation stopped as Ryan and I stepped into the kitchen and every head turned to look at us. Then it all turned into a flurry of activity as our family rushed us at once.

I lost track of Ryan as we were passed around, getting hugged and kissed and welcomed home by each member of the family and then finally, I was standing right in front of Caleb. We stared at each other for several long moments and I could see the tears pooling in his eyes. I opened my arms and he threw himself at me.

"Bubby," he whispered, burying his face in my neck.

"I'm here," I told him and then we both were crying and holding each other tightly. We were each very different men, with individual personalities and different tastes in everything from clothing to food choices, but at the same time, it was as if we were two parts of the same whole. We could feel what the other was feeling and often shared thoughts, so being separated felt like we'd been missing the other half of ourselves.

We stepped back, giving a little laugh as we wiped our eyes. The rest of our family was used to it so they'd busied themselves with serving up lunch and setting the table, allowing us a few minutes to ourselves.

"How long are you home for?" Caleb asked, and I could see the cautious look in his eyes as if he weren't sure he wanted to hear my answer. I saw several heads pop up, waiting for my response.

"Indefinitely. We're all ready for a break, so we're going to stay home and work on new songs, maybe put out a record or two. We may be here a couple of years before we're ready to head back out on tour," I told them. I heard Mom gasp and Caleb's face split into a wide smile.

"Are you serious?" he asked excitedly. I smiled back, nodding my head and then I started laughing as I was suddenly engulfed in a group hug.

I caught Ryan's eye as Landon pulled him into our hug. My husband had gone with me on my travels, supporting me and helping me achieve my dreams. Maybe it was time that the two of us looked into what other adventures we'd like to take together. Perhaps even starting a family of our own. Ryan's eyes widened as if he'd read my thoughts and the pure happiness in his eyes made my heart stutter.

Mom had made sandwiches and her homemade broccoli cheddar soup and we all talked as we ate, catching up on everything that had been going on with each other. When we were finished, we helped clear the dishes and then we pulled on our coats and shoes, so we could help Dad hang the lights outside.

"How many strands of lights are we putting up this year?" Landon asked.

"Just a few more than last year," he answered noncommittally.

"How many more, Dad?" Caleb asked suspiciously.

"I bought twenty more," he said with a sheepish grin and we all groaned. Ryan gave me a questioning look.

"Dad increases the number of lights on the house every Christmas. Last year, I think he used seventy-five strands. Planes were circling our house, looking for a place to land," I explained dramatically.

"It wasn't that bad," Mom said with a laugh. "Besides, we have grandbabies now and they deserve to have a bright and colorful Christmas." Ryan's head popped up at her words and he looked at me. I nodded at him and he turned to my brothers and their partners in crime.

"That reminds me, thank you so much for the warm welcome home gift you left in our living room." I watched as Landon, Micah, Caleb, and Giovanni busted out laughing, obviously pleased with themselves.

"The jokes on you though, because we already enjoyed several of the *ornaments*," I added. I laughed as Caleb and Landon scrunched up their noses at the thought of their brother using the sex toys they'd purchased.

"What are you boys talking about?" Dad asked suspiciously.

"Nothing," we all said in unison, feigning innocence. Dad narrowed his eyes at us, but then turned and headed outside. I reached up and playfully messed up Landon's hair and he tossed his arm around my shoulder as we made our way out to help our father.

With all of us working together, we were able to get the lights hung in just under two hours. It probably would've gone faster, but we were too busy laughing and having a good time to get it done any quicker. I caught Giovanni wearing a broad smile and I grinned at him.

"You look awfully happy," I said.

"I love this," he told me with a shrug.

"You love freezing your balls off?" I teased.

"No, that I could do without," he responded with a chuckle. "I meant all the rest of it. The closeness, the inside jokes that only members of a family would get. I haven't had that in a long time. When my parents died, and Julianna left, I thought I'd never have that again, that I'd be alone for the rest of my life." My heart hurt at the thought of the pain he'd been through.

"I'm glad you're part of our family." I spoke honestly. "You've given so much love to Caleb, but you've also brought more love and happiness to the rest of us too. You're a great guy, Giovanni, and I'm happy to have you as a brother." We spent a few more minutes talking and when I stepped away, Caleb grabbed me and pulled me into a fierce hug.

"What's that for?" I asked with a laugh.

"For being you," Caleb said with a shrug.

It was getting dark by the time we finished, and we bundled up the kids and brought them and Mom out to see our handiwork. Dad turned the lights on and we all oohed and aahed over the festive display. I had to admit, it looked amazing and we all took turns telling Dad that. Ryan stood behind me and wrapped his arms around my waist, kissing the side of my face.

"This is going to be the best Christmas yet," he said, and I smiled, leaning my head back on his chest.

We stood out there until our teeth started chattering and then we went inside to warm up with cups of hot chocolate, talking the whole way about what kind of competitions we should have and what price those who didn't win should have to pay. My parents had always made Christmas very special for us kids, but now with each of us having found our soulmates, I had to agree with Ryan. This Christmas was going to be the biggest and best.

CHAPTER
Seven

Caleb

"**O**KAY, HOLD STILL, WE'RE ALMOST done," I said.

I finished brushing the paint onto Sarah's hand and then pressed it gently onto the smooth surface of the cup. Once it was completely dry, I'd let her use markers to write her name on it then I'd coat the entire thing in glaze to keep it from peeling. I'd been trying to think of something special that Sarah could give to Giovanni for Christmas and Michelle had suggested a coffee mug with Sarah's handprint. I loved the idea and I knew Gio would too. Anything that had to do with our daughter tended to turn us into piles of goo.

"What a beautiful handprint. Daddy's going to be so surprised," I told her, and Sarah grinned up at me proudly. I grabbed her step stool and placed it in front of the sink then helped keep her steady as she climbed up to wash her hands.

"Sweetheart, have you seen Sarah?" I heard Gio call from down the hall. His voice sounded like it was getting closer and Sarah and I gave each other a wide-eyed look.

"We're in the kitchen, but you can't come in here yet," I hollered back.

"Why not? What are you two up to?" he asked, sounding amused. I could tell he was right outside the door, but I trusted him to not come in.

"We have surprises, Daddy," Sarah yelled and we both giggled.

"We'll be out in just a minute," I told him.

I washed out the brush and put it and the paint away and then Sarah helped me find a place to hide the mug where Gio wouldn't find it as it dried. When we were finished, we gave each other a high five and then went into the living room where we could hear the TV playing some old black-and-white Christmas movie. Gio was there, sitting on the couch and he smiled as we walked in. He opened up his arms and

Sarah climbed up onto his lap.

"So, are you going to tell me what you and Dad were doing in the kitchen?" Gio asked her.

"No, Daddy. It's a surprise," she said with a giggle.

"Are you sure?" he asked.

"Quit trying to coerce our daughter," I said with a laugh as I plopped down on the couch beside them. "You'll have to wait until Christmas morning to get your surprise."

Gio stuck out his bottom lip in an adorable pout and I couldn't resist leaning over to kiss it. He kissed me back then gave Sarah a kiss on the cheek before blowing into her neck and making her squeal in delight as it tickled her. My phone rang as he began to tickle her ribs and I dug it out of my back pocket to answer it.

"Hello?" I answered with a laugh.

"What in the world is going on there?" Michelle asked, obviously hearing the loud noises through the phone.

"Tickle war," I told her.

"Oh, sounds like fun! Tell my niece to fight dirty," she said with a laugh.

"I'll come to her defense if I need to," I assured her with a chuckle.

"Good. Now, I'm calling for a reason. We need you guys to get over to Mom and Dad's place as soon as possible," she informed me.

"Why? What's up?" I asked.

"It's competition time," she said deviously.

"Ugh! Seriously? My legs are still sore from climbing that hill over and over in the sled-riding competition and I'm just starting to feel my feet after being outside for four hours yesterday for the snow-man-building competition," I teasingly complained. The truth was, Gio and I had both had a blast, even if we'd lost both challenges.

"Oh, quit your whining. You and Carter are younger than me and I'm not complaining," Michelle pointed out.

"Are you even going to tell me what the competition is?" I asked.

"Nope. You'll find out along with everyone else when they get here," she teased.

"Fine, we'll be there soon," I said.

"Another competition?" Gio asked as I hung up.

"Yeah, I'm sorry. I can call her back if you'd rather just stay in tonight," I offered.

"No way! We took it easy on them the last couple of times. It's time we kick some Greene as…" I cut him off with a loud cough and nodded my head at our daughter who was still on his lap, watching the TV. "Bootay," Gio finished with a smile. I laughed and grabbed him by the back of the neck, so I could pull him forward for a kiss.

Thirty minutes later, we opened the door to my parents' house and stepped into a room full of chaos and noise. More chaos and noise than was typical when my family would get together. A quick look around explained why. Joining my siblings and their spouses was also Akio and Morgan, Rylie and Lachlan, and Hudson, Isaac, and Matt.

"Finally, everybody's here. Now we can get this thing started," Emma said.

"What thing? You still haven't told us what we're doing," Landon said, looking at our sister suspiciously.

"If you'll all take a seat, we'll explain," Michelle told him, stepping forward to stand beside Emma.

Gio finished helping Sarah out of her coat and boots and then released her to go to my mom who took her by the hand and led her into the kitchen. The rest of us took a seat as instructed and looked up at my sisters expectantly. They were nearly vibrating with excitement as they stood in front of us and my interest was piqued. If my sisters had cooked up a plan together, it was bound to be good.

"I've already explained to the new recruits that it's a tradition for us to hold competitions each year over the holidays and they've agreed to join us," Emma explained, holding a clipboard in her hands. I glanced around the room and saw our friends shaking their heads and smiling. They probably thought we were crazy, but then again, they fit right in with us, so I guess the same could be said about them.

"Emma and I were talking one day and decided that we needed to step things up this year. So, we put our heads together and came up with a new competition that we think will be a lot of fun," Michelle said. The devious grin she and Emma exchanged had me wondering exactly what we were getting ourselves into.

"Why do I have the feeling I'm going to regret this?" Ryan teased.

"Don't worry, Superman. I'll protect you," Carter told his husband.

I chuckled when I saw the blush that crept up Ryan's neck. He'd never gotten used to the nickname my brother gave him after rescuing him when our restaurant caught fire with Carter inside, but Carter insisted that Ryan was his hero and the nickname had stuck. Ryan opened his mouth to say something, but Carter leaned over and gave him a kiss, effectively cutting off his response. A wave of happiness washed over me, and I knew I was experiencing Carter's feelings as he kissed his husband.

"Okay, you two. Let's find out what we have to do," I said gruffly, wanting to stop them before I experienced more…heated feelings my brother would start having for his husband. Carter turned and gave me a smug look, knowing exactly why I'd stopped them.

"Don't worry, we'll get even," Gio whispered in my ear and my laugh made Carter narrow his eyes at me.

"Anyway, back to the competition," Emma said, and I turned my attention back on my sisters, giving them an apologetic look. She glanced around to make sure she had everyone's attention. Satisfied, she announced, "We're heading into the city for a scavenger hunt." We all looked around at each other, some of us sitting up as we waited to hear more.

"Michelle and I are the captains and we've divided everyone into two teams. Team One will be me and Mark, Caleb and Giovanni, Morgan and Akio, Hudson, Isaac, and Matt," Emma told us, reading the names off the list in her hand. We all grinned at each other and Matt and I bumped fists.

"Team Two consists of me and Jason, Carter and

Ryan, Landon and Micah, and Rylie and Lachlan." Michelle had just finished reading off the names when Landon spoke up.

"That's not fair, they have an extra person," he complained. "Plus, we have Carter. That's an automatic handicap," he added with a smirk.

"Hey now! I can win this thing with my hands tied behind my back," Carter informed him pompously.

"Let's keep what you do in the bedroom out of this," Rylie teased. We all started laughing when Carter flipped his middle finger up at him.

"I'd like to say that I'm sorry that my falling in love with two men instead of one is causing problems, but I'm just not," Isaac added with a playful shrug. Hudson and Matt sat on either side of him, grinning like fools. It was obvious that none of them were sorry in the least, not that they had any reason to be. They knew our teasing was all done in good fun.

"We already took into account the added person advantage and Team Two has already been awarded a five-point start," Michelle informed us all.

"How this works is simple. Each team will be provided a matching list of items that are to be found. It's a long list and impossible to find every item in the time allotted. That said, you should choose wisely which items are worth your time because as you will see, every item is worth a different amount of points," Emma said as she passed a copy of the list to each person.

"You must work as a team to gather each item, no dividing up the list. And, purchasing any item is strictly forbidden. You're going to have to get creative to obtain your goods. Each team will have three hours to gather as many things from the list as you can and bring them back here, where we will tally the points and declare a winner," Michelle added.

We all began scanning the pages as soon as we got them, except for Micah who got up to make a phone call. I could hear laughter and murmuring as we saw a range of things, from the innocent child's teddy bear, to the not-so-innocent woman's thong. My eyebrows raised at that one and I glanced up at my sisters who looked quite pleased with themselves. I had to admit, they'd come up with a great challenge and I was sure we'd all have fun doing it.

"One other thing," Emma said and we all settled down so we could listen. "The losing team will be required to carol around the neighborhood tonight wearing special costumes." Michelle walked to the hall closet and brought back a bag. From it, she pulled green hats, ridiculous green shoes and red and white striped tights in an assortment of sizes. There was also green shorts and shirts and floppy ears attached to a headband.

"Elves? We have to dress as elves and go door to door singing Christmas carols?" Carter groaned, his face turning pale. I knew he was picturing all the videos of him that would be posted all over social media.

"As your team captain and someone who would have to do it right along with you, I suggest you don't lose," Michelle said, clapping him on the shoulder. Carter rolled his eyes as she walked away and I chuckled.

"Okay, you have about ten minutes to split up into your teams and strategize," Emma announced and we all stood up, huddling in separate corners of the living room as each team developed a game plan.

"I'll be back in a minute," I whispered to Gio. He gave me a nod before giving his attention to our teammates.

I headed into the kitchen in search of my daughter. Dad smiled as I walked in. He was wearing an apron and was just pulling a batch of sugar cookies out of the oven. Mom and Sarah were at the table and when they looked at me, I saw that Sarah was wearing a red smile across her face from the iced cookie she'd been eating.

"It looks like you guys are having fun in here," I said, bending down and stealing a bite of cookie. Sarah giggled as she pulled the cookie away.

"We are. We're making cookies for Santa and then we thought we'd take the kids to see him at the mall," Mom said.

"Are you sure you don't mind keeping Sarah with you while we do this?" I asked. Dad barked out a laugh.

"Are you kidding? We live for this. If you hadn't come by with our granddaughter, we were going to come and steal her anyway," he joked. I looked to my mother who nodded her head in confirmation.

"Okay, if you're sure," I said with a laugh.

"We're sure, honey. Go, have fun," Mom said. I hugged all three of them and then hurried back out to the living room where everyone was putting on their coats.

"Everything alright with Sarah?" Gio asked, handing me my coat and gloves.

"Yeah, she's on her way to a sugar rush right now and then she and my parents and the babies are going to see Santa." Gio laughed at my description then wrapped my scarf around me and gave me a kiss.

"Alright, when I say go, we'll have three hours. Good luck, everyone, and may the best team, in other words, *my team*, win," Michelle joked. "Aaaaand Go!"

We all rushed out the door and scrambled into our cars. Hudson, Isaac, and Matt jumped into the back of our car while Morgan and Akio shared a ride with Emma and Mark. Our team made it out of the driveway first, but the other team was right on our heels as we all headed back to the city.

"Hey, Emma." I turned in my seat to see Matt on his phone. He held it away from him and put it on speaker so we all could hear. "I was wondering, is there a rule about how many items you can get from one place?"

"No, we never made that a rule, so I guess you can get as much as you want. What have you got in mind?" she asked.

"Let's head to Agape House," he said with a mischievous grin.

A broad smile spread across my face and I reached back to bump fists with my friend as Isaac got on his phone and called Allison, who was working at Agape House that day, to explain to her what was going on.

By the time we got there, she had already

gathered the teens into a group. They were talking excitedly as we walked in, all of them eager to help. Emma read the list out loud, carefully omitting the more adult items and the kids rushed off to their rooms to retrieve the things they wanted to contribute.

Ten minutes later we had over twenty items crossed off our list, which we promised to return as soon as the competition was over. The kids helped us to our cars with our loot and gave us hugs, cheering for us as we pulled out of the parking lot. With everything we'd already collected, we were feeling pretty confident that we'd win this competition.

CHAPTER
Eight

Micah

THE STREETS AND SIDEWALKS WERE crowded with people finishing their last-minute Christmas shopping and I breathed a sigh of relief, knowing that the men I had called to accompany us would keep my more famous friends and family members protected from overzealous fans.

So far, people had been courteous, only asking for an autograph or a quick picture and then leaving us to our fun, but I wasn't willing to take any chances. I'd also sent a couple of guys to meet up with Caleb's team since he was often mistaken for Carter. We walked into a busy coffee shop and looked around.

"Play along," Landon said, giving me a wink as he took my hand and pulled me behind him. "Excuse me," he said to a man and woman sitting at a nearby table.

The couple looked up at him curiously. Landon smiled at them and I had to hide my grin when the woman began to blush, her jaw dropping as she stared at my husband. I almost felt sorry for her because I knew what it did to *me* every time he turned that megawatt smile in my direction, and I was allowed to do something about it. I couldn't imagine how difficult it must be to come face-to-face with the gorgeous man and not be able to touch. The fact that he didn't realize the effect he had on people made him even more alluring.

"My husband and I are on our way to his office Christmas party and he just now mentioned that he was supposed to wear a Christmas sweater." Landon rolled his eyes, sighing dramatically. "He just started working there and is trying to fit in, but well, I'm sure you know how forgetful our men can get sometimes and now he's going to show up and be the only employee there without a festive shirt." I bit back a laugh as the woman nodded her head as if she knew exactly what Landon was talking about.

"Give him your sweater, dear," she told her husband. He looked at her in surprise.

"What? You can't be serious," he said.

"Oh, that thing is hideous anyway," she responded, gesturing to the bright red sweater that had a picture of Santa waving a wad of single dollar bills in the air as he watched a female elf swinging on a stripper pole. The caption above it read "Miss Candy Cane was the most popular elf at the North Pole."

"But I love this sweater," he protested.

"You only love it because your mother got it for you which is even more wrong than what's on it," she said, rolling her eyes.

The man grumbled something I couldn't hear, but he pulled the sweater over his head, leaving him in just a turtleneck. Landon and I thanked the couple profusely and then rushed to the door where the rest of our team was waiting.

"One ugly Christmas sweater for twenty points," Landon announced as we stepped out onto the sidewalk. He shared high fives with our teammates and then turned to me and grinned sheepishly.

"So, I'm the forgetful husband, huh?" I said, crossing my arms over my chest and pretending to glare at him.

"I didn't mean it, baby," Landon purred, moving

in close and wrapping his arms around my waist.

"Still, I think I'll make you pay for that when we get home," I whispered in his ear.

Landon pulled back, swallowing thickly as he searched my face. He looked almost nervous and I frowned in concern. What possible reason would Landon have to be nervous with me? He opened his mouth to say something, but before he got the chance, Carter interrupted.

"I've got a great idea. We're about to get a lot of points," he said, waving the list in the air with a triumphant smile.

He grabbed Rylie by the arm and turned, talking to his friend as they walked quickly down the sidewalk. The rest of us looked at each other questioningly then shrugged our shoulders and hurried to catch up. A half a block further, they stopped near a couple of street performers who were playing outside a bar. The two young men were each playing guitar and one was singing into a microphone. Despite their amazing voices, the guitar case which sat opened in front of them was nearly empty except for a few wadded-up dollar bills and some change.

We listened as they finished their song and then Carter and Rylie walked up to them. It was almost comical to see their reactions as the famous drummer and lead singer approached them. Carter spoke to them for a few seconds and the two guys smiled, nodding their heads excitedly.

"Hey, everybody! How are you all doing?" Carter said as he turned and stepped up to the microphone.

I looked around when what had been a very small crowd quickly grew as people began to recognize the men from one of the world's hottest bands. Some people pulled their phones out and began recording and my body went on high alert. I searched the crowd for my men and saw them moving in close, one standing to the right of Carter and Rylie and the other, just to the left. I grabbed Landon's hand to keep him near and pushed my way to the front, thinking of all the ways I was going to kill Carter when this was over.

"I hope you're having a great time getting ready for Christmas. Rocko and I just got back in town to spend some time with our families and we heard the awesome music being played by our friends, Jared and Bryce." The two guys raised their hands in the air and smiled widely as the crowd cheered.

"We'd like to play a couple songs for you, if that's alright, and if you like what you hear, maybe you can toss some change into the case for our friends," Rylie added.

The then very large crowd cheered again as Jared and Bryce began to play and Rylie and Carter shared the microphone, belting out lively renditions of "Jingle Bell Rock" and "Last Christmas," followed by "Santa Claus Is Comin' To Town." By the time they'd finished, the police had arrived to help with the crowd and the guitar case was overflowing with cash.

Carter and Rylie shook hands with the two other musicians and I wasn't surprised when both Lachlan and my husband walked up to them, handing them their cards. I didn't know all that much about music, but even I had been impressed with the way they'd held their own, despite the crowd and the nerves they must have felt, playing with such giants in the industry. Lachlan called for his driver and I nodded to my men who helped me secure our group and get them safely into the limo as it pulled up.

"What the hell was that?" Ryan and I both yelled at the same time as soon as the door was shut. Carter and Rylie exchanged a look and then Rylie pulled a couple of things out of his pocket. He smiled as he held them up in the air and I took a closer look, my jaw dropping when I realized it was a woman's lace bra and a bright yellow thong.

"Oh, and don't forget the candy cane-flavored

condom I got. I believe that was worth two hundred points," Carter added smugly.

"How the hell did you get those?" Jason asked.

"They threw them into the guitar case," Rylie answered.

"But how did you know they'd do that?" he pressed further.

"It happens all the time. You'd be surprised what people toss on stage during a concert," Carter told him, shrugging his shoulders like it was no big deal.

"That's disturbing," Michelle muttered. "Impressive, but disturbing all the same."

"Here," Lachlan said, pulling a plastic bag from a hidden compartment inside the limo and handing it to Rylie to drop the undergarments into. "And use this," he told his husband, passing him a bottle of hand sanitizer. Rylie laughed, but squirted the liquid into his hand anyway.

After a slight detour where Lachlan used his British accent to woo a preacher's wife out of the baby Jesus from the Nativity scene in front of the church, we finally made it back to the house with only minutes to spare. We filed inside and deposited our treasures onto the living room floor while the other team did the same.

We all sat around the dining room

table, warming up over cups of coffee and a plate of Christmas cookies while Kathy and Rick tallied up the scores. We shared stories of how we'd acquired some of our items, laughing at some of the more creative ploys. Eventually, Landon's parents walked in and we looked at them anxiously as we waited to hear who had won.

"Well, it was a pretty close call. Team One brought in a lot of items, but Team Two had a few high scoring items," Rick said. "In the end, the competition was won by just ten points." It was completely quiet as we all leaned closer.

"And the winner is... Team Two," Kathy declared, sounding like a game show announcer. "Michelle, Jason, Carter, Ryan, Landon, Micah, Rylie and Lachlan, you may take a bow and present the losing team with their ears."

We whooped and hollered then bowed dramatically to the teasing boos of our opponents. Then, we each took a pair of elf ears from Kathy and handed them out to the members of the opposite team. But, like the good sports they were, they quickly changed into their elf costumes and trudged through the neighborhood, knocking on doors and singing Christmas carols while our team followed along, recording the entire thing on our phones.

All in all, it had been a fun-filled day and as we ate the pizzas that Kathy had ordered, we each agreed that Michelle and Emma should be in charge of planning any future competitions. Competitions which would also include our friends from then on.

An hour later, Landon and I walked through our front door. He'd been rather quiet on the way home and I wondered if it had to do with the look he'd given me back in front of the coffee shop. It was obvious that something was on his mind and I intended to get to the bottom of it. Laying my keys on the table and making sure the door was locked, I followed him down the hallway to our room. When I got there, he had already taken his shirt off and was staring down at the material in his hands.

"A penny for your thoughts," I said, leaning against the doorway. He jumped and turned to me with a startled look.

"What?" he asked. I walked forward until I was standing directly in front of him.

"I can tell something's bothering you and I'd like to know what it is," I told him, lifting his chin so he'd look at me. "Is it your anxiety? Did something happen to trigger it?" It had been a long time since Landon had suffered a panic attack and his therapist was pleased with his progress, but I knew that there was always a chance that something could set him back.

"No, it's nothing like that. I promise," he rushed to assure me, reaching his hands up to cradle my face.

"Then what is it? You know you can talk to me about anything," I reminded him. Landon puffed his cheeks and let out a long, slow breath.

"I know. It's just something I've been thinking about..." he trailed off, shrugging his shoulders.

"Tell me," I pleaded. He pulled out of my grasp and began pacing the floor in front of me.

"It's not that I'm not happy with the way things are between us, because trust me, I am. It's just that lately I've been curious," he stated.

"Curious about what?" I asked, my voice cracking at the end.

Did Landon want to try an open marriage? Did he want to invite a third into our relationship? My mind swirled with agonizing images of Landon in the arms of another man. I didn't have a problem with triads, in fact, I was very happy that Hudson, Isaac, and Matt had fallen in love with each other, but I wasn't built that way. I didn't think it would be possible for me to share Landon without it totally destroying me.

Landon stared at me, looking very vulnerable and I saw a tremor go through him. I grabbed him into my arms and held him close, rubbing soothing circles over the smooth skin of his back. Right then, I knew that I would give Landon anything he asked for, no matter how much it might hurt me. His happiness was the only thing that mattered and if he needed something beyond what I alone could offer him, then I'd make sure he got it.

"Curious about what?" I repeated, that time in a steady voice.

"About what it would be like…to top you," he whispered, dropping his head onto my shoulder. It took a moment for his words to sink in and then I was grinning and pulling him back so I could see his face.

"Is that all?" I asked, feeling my shoulders sag as the tension left my body.

"Well, yeah. It's just that I didn't know how you'd feel about it and I didn't want you to think that I was unhappy with our sex life, because I'm not. At all," he stressed.

"As long as you don't want anyone else, then I'm happy," I said, feeling a bit giddy.

"Anyone else? What are you talking about?" he asked, looking disgusted by the idea.

"Nothing, never mind," I said, leaning in to kiss him soundly.

Landon sagged against me as I deepened the kiss, sweeping my tongue over the roof of his mouth and sucking on his tongue. I felt his cock grow hard against my thigh and I reached down, cupping it through his jeans. Landon moaned and tilted his head back, so I could trail my lips down his throat, but then I pulled back. He swayed for a moment and I held onto his arms to steady him, smirking at the effect I'd had on him. *How could I have doubted the chemistry between us for even a second?*

"Why did you stop?" He opened his eyes, blinking at me.

"Because tonight, we're doing things a little differently," I told him. Landon licked his lips, obviously liking the idea. "Just so you know, I've never been opposed to having you top," I continued, but Landon looked at me as if he were still unsure.

"When we first got together, we both fulfilled a need in each other," I explained. "I needed to have control because so many things in my life had been out of my control for far too long, and you needed someone else to take control, to make the decisions that you were just too tired to make. But we're different now. We've grown as individuals and as a couple. We've continued things the way they've been because we enjoy them, not because we necessarily need them anymore." I watched as a small smile of understanding lifted the corners of his mouth and I smiled back.

"I want to share *everything* with you, Landon, including feeling you inside me." He gasped at that and his eyes darkened with lust. Landon tracked my movements as I took another step back and pulled my shirt over my head, letting it drop to the floor. His hands reached out and stopped me as I reached for my belt.

"I want to do that," he whispered.

His hands were steady, the look in his eyes sure as he unfastened the buckle, pulling the leather from my pants and tossing it to the floor with a loud clank. Next, he unbuttoned my pants and I hissed when his knuckles grazed my erection as he slowly lowered my zipper. His fingers teased along the waistband of my briefs, just barely dipping in, and my hands fisted at my sides as I fought the urge to throw him on the bed and sink my cock into his succulent body. This night was a new first for us, and I was determined to stay the course.

My pulse burned through my veins as Landon sank to his knees, staring up at me as he reached for my pants and briefs and lowered both of them over my hips and down my legs. I kicked them off then held my breath, waiting to see what he'd do next. I didn't have to wait long as he used the flat of his tongue to lick a line from the base of my cock to the tip. He moaned as he tasted the pre-cum that leaked from the head and I reached for him, running my fingers through his hair and gently urging him on.

He sucked me into his mouth and my knees nearly buckled at the feel of his warm, wet mouth surrounding my cock. His head bobbed up and down expertly, knowing exactly what to do to bring me the greatest pleasure. I automatically tensed as I felt him spread my cheeks and a wet finger traced a line through my crack. Landon halted his movements and peered up at me, releasing my cock from his mouth.

"Do you trust me?" he asked.

"Yes," I answered swiftly. There was no reason to hesitate. I trusted Landon with my life.

"Then trust me to make you feel as good as you always make me feel," he whispered. I nodded my head. "Get on the bed." A shiver swept through me at the authority in my lover's voice. I liked that side of him. Of course, I liked every side of my husband.

I lay on the bed and scooted until my head

reached the pillows. Placing my hands behind my head in a leisurely manner, I enjoyed the show as Landon finished undressing himself, exposing miles of flawless skin over toned muscles. He walked to the side of the bed and pulled a bottle of lube from the table drawer then he crawled onto the bed and between my spread thighs with an almost feral grin. He licked his lips as he looked over my body, as if deciding where to start.

Finally, he dropped to his stomach and pushed my legs up toward my chest. I held the backs of my knees as he instructed and gasped when I felt Landon's firm hands spreading my cheeks apart. It felt a bit strange, exposing that part of myself to him, but Landon calmed my nerves by whispering words of encouragement and praise until all I wanted was for him to touch me. His tongue flicked out and circled my hole and I nearly shot off the bed as nerves I'd never felt before sprang to life like live wires.

Landon chuckled and then pursed his lips, blowing a cooling breath against my hole. It was in such opposition of my feverish skin that my mind swirled, trying to make sense of the foreign sensations. My hands went to his hair as he continued to lick and taste that part of me that had never known anyone else. I writhed on the bed, torn between never wanting him to stop and feeling as if I needed more.

I felt his thumb press against my entrance and all I could think was, "Thank God!" I heard the cap from the bottle of lube snap open and instinctively, I pulled my knees up, leaving myself open to him and he poured it over his finger, wetting it thoroughly before easing it inside me. It felt odd at first, but I forced myself to relax. Soon, his entire finger was in and he began to move it slowly, in and out of me, stretching me and preparing me to take his cock.

He added another finger and I breathed through the discomfort, but then he twisted his wrist and I had to fight back a scream. *Holy shit! So, that's what a prostate massage feels like.* His voice sounded far away as my pulse rushed through my ears.

"Micah, are you okay?" Somehow, I registered his concern, so I assured him the only way I could think of in my warbled mental state.

"Do that again," I gasped. I heard his deep rumble of laughter, but he did as I asked, and I closed my eyes, enjoying the stars that burned behind my lids and the lightning that swept through my body. Landon continued to work me open until I was begging him to please, fuck me.

He sat up and slicked his cock with lube, then he lay over me, holding himself up with one arm while the other hand reached between us to line himself up. A tiny sliver of fear, a fear of the unknown, raced down my spine. I had never bottomed before, never trusted anyone enough for that kind of intimacy, but Landon knew that already and I could see the understanding in his eyes as he gazed down at me, along with all the love and tenderness he felt for me.

"I love you more than anything else in the world," he whispered, and I felt all my fears leave my body, completely eclipsed by this man and the way he made me feel. I placed my hands on either side of his face and leaned up, so I could press a kiss against his lips.

"I'm ready, baby. Let me feel you," I said.

I bit my lip against the pressure, but Landon moved slowly, being very careful with me as he eased inside. He stared into my eyes the entire time and I watched the range of emotions that flitted across his face. Everything from utter joy to unquestionable devotion showed in his expression and I nearly wept with my love for him.

We kissed as he began to move inside me and I groaned as all the pain was replaced with absolute ecstasy. I pulled my knees up to my chest as he began to thrust harder and I slipped my hand between us, taking my cock and pumping it in my tight fist.

"You feel so good. I don't know how much longer I can last," Landon groaned.

"It's okay. I'm right there with you," I panted. I could already feel my balls drawing up tight as my cock leaked all over my stomach.

Landon adjusted his position and gave me a deep thrust, nailing my prostate perfectly and I screamed his name as cum shot from my cock, splattering my chest. His body stiffened above me and with one last push, I could feel his hot seed as it filled me.

He collapsed on top of me, completely spent and I wrapped my arms around him, holding him as close as possible. There were no words to describe how much love I felt for him or how in awe I was over everything that had just happened. So, I didn't even try. I simply held him, enjoying the pounding of his heart against my chest and the feel of his warm breath against my neck.

CHAPTER
Nine

Isaac

I SAT AT THE TABLE, LISTENING TO THE CHATTER around me as I strung blue and white beads onto a wire. I'd already succeeded in making three others and when I was finished, I was going to wrap them around each other in the middle to make a snowflake. Hopefully anyway, I wasn't the craftiest person in the world. Either way, I figured it would look pretty hanging on the Christmas tree with colorful lights shining through the iridescent beads.

It was a mindless task and I smiled as I listened to the kids laughing and joking with one another as we made ornaments for the enormous tree that the

Greenes had brought to the center. It had been a surprise, one that brought smiles to the kids' faces, and they'd immediately started making plans for where to place it so they could all enjoy it. It was finally decided that it would go in the spacious dining room so they could see it as they ate their meals and played games.

They had the next two weeks off school for Christmas break and there was an excited buzz in the air. I was happy to see that most of the kids were looking forward to the holidays. It wasn't easy to spend Christmas away from home, but considering most of their home lives had consisted of constant pain and anguish, they seemed relieved to be around people who truly cared about them and wanted what was best for them.

That was largely due to Matt's influence. As the owner of the center, he'd always treated every kid that walked through the doors like they were important, like they were family. I knew because he'd done the same for me. Hudson and I had followed his lead and the three of us worked hard to make sure every kid was included and cared for.

I tied off the end of my wire and attempted to wrap the beaded wires around each other, but it ended up looking completely lopsided, almost like a person in a flowing skirt with their arms spread to the side.

"You need some help with your snowflake?" someone whispered into my ear and a delicious shiver ran up my neck.

I turned and looked into the warm, brown eyes of my husband. My eyes flitted down to the set of plump lips and I sighed as I remembered how those lips felt pressed against mine. Those same lips lifted in a smirk and Hudson's eyes danced in amusement knowing the path my thoughts had taken.

"What?" I asked as I struggled to remember his question.

"Your snowflake. Do you need help putting it together?" he asked, gesturing toward my hands.

I looked down, suddenly remembering the ornament I had been working on. Hudson and Matt knew the effect they had on me and they seemed to get great pleasure from scrambling my brain. Fortunately, I knew exactly how to do the same to them, so they weren't the only ones who could have fun.

"No, I've decided I like it best as a snow fairy," I told him, curving the two wires to the sides upward so they'd look more like arms.

"I like it too," Hudson said, giving me a quick

kiss. A chorus of catcalls and whistles sounded nearby and we looked over to see the kids watching us.

"Alright, show's over. That tree is huge and there are a lot of bare spots that still need to be filled," he told them with a laugh.

The kids were used to seeing Hudson, Matt, and me being appropriately affectionate in front of them. We'd decided long ago not to hide our feelings from them. Most of them had never seen a healthy, loving, and committed relationship and we felt that they needed role models so that they would know what to look for when they entered relationships of their own. That didn't mean that they didn't like to give us a hard time about it though.

"You ready to go?" Hudson asked, and I glanced down at my watch, realizing how late it had gotten.

"Yeah, we'd better get a move on," I agreed.

I quickly scooped up the leftover beads and put them back in the plastic storage case I had taken them from, then attached a hook to my snow fairy and hung her on the tree. I grabbed my coat from my office and shrugged it on as I walked past the front desk, saying goodbye to Allison.

A thrill shot through me when I saw Hudson waiting for me at the front door. His hand held just the right amount of pressure as he placed it on my lower back and guided me across the parking lot and into our car. He climbed into the driver seat and immediately pulled me towards him, taking my mouth in a searing kiss that left me breathless and aching for more. The snow had continued to fall while we'd been at work, leaving the windows covered in a thick blanket. It gave the illusion of being totally secluded, shielded from the rest of the world.

Hudson's tongue delved inside my mouth, tasting, searching and demanding in its urgency. My hands went around the back of his neck, pulling him closer and refusing to let him retreat. My head spun with the lack of oxygen and the love I felt for him and I whimpered as he pulled away, despite my hold on him.

"I've been dying to do that ever since you crawled out of our bed this morning." Hudson's voice was deep and sounded strained and I knew I wasn't the only one wishing we could take things farther. Unfortunately, we were in the parking lot of a youth center and besides that, we had things we needed to get done before our company arrived.

"Later," I whispered, that one word holding the promise of pleasures yet to come, and allowing us to hold off on the desire that threatened to choke us.

Hudson nodded his head once then shook it, as

if to clear it, before turning the wipers on to clear the windshield and backing out of the parking space. I tried to discreetly adjust my hardened cock inside my slacks, but Hudson's low groan told me that he'd caught my movement. I smirked as I looked out my window, pleased with his reaction. There was no denying that the three of us, whether all together or separately, were combustible; and while it left us feeling frustrated when we couldn't do anything about it, I wouldn't change it for the world.

We pulled into the driveway of our home and Hudson turned off the car. He grabbed the groceries we'd picked up along the way in one hand and then reached his other out to me as we walked up the drive and into the house.

I sighed as the warmth inside the house began to soak into my bones, thawing me out. Matt walked into the room as we were taking off our coats and I felt the same fluttering I always got in my stomach whenever he was near. He smiled as he walked over and kissed me, nibbling my lower lip and sending ripples of pleasure down my spine.

I watched through hooded eyes as Matt turned to Hudson, holding onto his biceps as the two of them used their mouths to reconnect after the long day apart. My cock perked up again at the luscious sight of my men kissing and I scowled. We had several hours before I could devour them the way I wanted, and I didn't need my balls getting any bluer in the meantime.

"Okay, enough of that. Everyone needs to keep their hands and their lips to themselves. At least until we get through dinner and have the place to ourselves again," I scolded, pointing a finger at each of them. Matt cocked his head at me and then spoke to Hudson, who was regarding me with obvious amusement.

"At work?" Matt asked.

"In the car," Hudson responded. I rolled my eyes as the two of them bumped their fists together.

"You two are impossible," I said, shaking my head as I started to walk off.

Matt grabbed me by the arm and spun me back around so our chests brushed against each other and Hudson moved up behind me, the two of them effectively trapping me between their bodies. Not that I minded one little bit. In fact, I had to bite down on my cheek to suppress my grin.

"I'm sorry, we were being unfair," Hudson said as he placed a gentle kiss on the side of my head.

"We just can't seem to help ourselves when it comes to you. You always respond so beautifully,"

Matt whispered. He tilted my chin up and brushed his lips over mine. Hudson leaned forward and the three of us shared a kiss that felt as natural as breathing. Matt broke the kiss before we could get carried away again and we all smiled at each other.

"Come on, we better get started on dinner," Hudson said. He grabbed the groceries that he'd set by the front door and Matt and I followed him into the kitchen.

Two hours later, the doorbell rang, and Matt hurried to answer it. He smiled when he found his parents on the other side and he ushered them in, hugging and kissing them both. Matt's parents lived a couple hours away, so Hudson and I had only met them once before, at our wedding, but they were every bit as kind and loving as Matt had described. His mom's eyes lit up when she saw me and Hudson standing a few feet behind her son, and soon we were being swept up in fierce hugs as well.

We had just settled down in the living room to talk when the doorbell rang again. That time, it was Hudson's family, his sister Aysha, her boyfriend, Drew, and her son, Nicholas. They filed into the living room, hugging each of us and shaking hands with Matt's parents.

Our blended family fit so perfectly together that

it was as if they'd always known each other. Over dinner, Aysha and Matt's mother exchanged tales about Matt and Hudson when they were little boys. Hudson and Matt each glared at me as I had the women promise to bring photo albums the next time we were all together. Matt's dad and Drew each liked to golf and soon they were off talking about their favorite courses to play.

My eyes traveled around the table, taking in each person as they talked animatedly and laughed with each other. There was so much love in that room that it was hard to believe that just the year before, I had spent Christmas all alone in my run-down apartment. I'd spent most of the day with the kids at Agape House, but afterward, I returned home to a cold, loveless existence. Now, my life was rich and full, and I had more love in my life than I knew what to do with at times. I rubbed a hand over my chest as I suddenly felt a painful ache there.

I got up, making an excuse that I needed to use the restroom and made my escape, hopefully before anyone could notice the tears in my eyes. I closed the door to the bathroom and leaned against it, letting out a silent sob against the pain in my chest. My head hung forward as tears streamed down my cheeks and my hands fisted at my sides. A gentle knock at the door startled me and I jumped.

"Just a second," I called out. I rushed over to the sink and turned on the faucet, splashing cold water on my face then I grabbed a towel and wiped it dry. The reflection in the mirror showed red-rimmed eyes and a blotchy complexion. One look at me and my men would know that I'd been crying.

"Isaac, will you let us in?" Matt asked softly through the door. My shoulders slumped as I realized that there was no use hiding my feelings. Matt and Hudson knew me better than anyone else in the world. With a resigned sigh, I opened the door.

"Oh, baby. What is it?" Matt tilted my chin up, so he could see my face. Without waiting for an answer, he grabbed me into his arms, hugging me to him. I saw Hudson's concerned face over Matt's shoulder and a fresh wave of tears blurred my vision.

"I'm sorry, I'm not trying to spoil this fabulous evening," I said, brushing my tears away angrily. Matt never let go of me, but he moved to the side so that Hudson could step into the room as well.

"Don't apologize. We love you, and if something's bothering you we want to know what it is. Did someone say something to upset you?" Hudson asked, a frown marring his beautiful face as his arms joined Matt's around my waist.

"No, not at all," I told them, shaking my head for emphasis. "Everyone's been absolutely wonderful. We've been having so much fun and everyone's so happy."

"So, what's the problem?" Matt pressed.

"*That's* the problem," Hudson answered for me. I wasn't sure if it was the therapist in him or what, but sometimes it seemed as if he could read our minds.

"You're worried about Zane," Matt said as understanding dawned on his face. I nodded my head.

"I was thinking about how different my life is now compared to last year," I explained to them. "I have all this love and family in my life now, but just last year I went home to an empty apartment. There was no one to greet me at the door with kisses or to laugh with as we cooked a meal together. And then, I started to wonder..." My voice trailed off.

"You wondered if Zane has anyone," Matt finished for me. A sob tore through me and I buried my face in Matt's chest. He and Hudson held me tightly, letting me cry until I just couldn't cry anymore. Hudson wet a washcloth and began wiping the tears from my face.

"Listen to me. Zane is out there somewhere and there's no way for us to know if he has anyone special in his life, but from everything you've told us about him, I can guarantee one thing." Hudson finished cleaning my face and then he tossed the cloth into the sink. "I guarantee that he's thinking about you too and wondering what you're doing. He's probably thinking about the brother he loves more than his own life and he knows that no matter what else is going on in his life, there's at least one person out there that loves him. You."

A smile spread across my face at his words. Hudson was right. No matter how many miles were between us, or how many years since we'd seen each other, I knew that Zane loved me, and he knew that I loved him. I just needed to have faith that Micah's man would be able to find him and bring him back.

"And I bet Zane will be enjoying Christmas with us next year," Matt added, and I spread my arms out, hugging them both.

"Thank you both so much. I honestly don't know what I'd ever do without the two of you," I told them.

"That's something you'll never have to find out," Hudson assured me. The three of us shared a kiss until a pounding at the door caused us to jump apart in surprise.

"You guys, I have to go pee," Nicholas yelled through the door and we started laughing, opening the door and ushering the boy inside before he could have an accident.

I followed my men back down the hallway and joined the rest of our family, determined to have a lovely Christmas and spend it counting all of my blessings. With any luck, I'd soon be able to add having my brother back to my list.

CHAPTER
Ten

Carter

I STARED LAZILY AT THE SNOW COMING DOWN outside. It had been falling steadily for several days, and the weathermen were reporting around eight to ten inches had accumulated so far. The wind blew noisily just beyond that thin pane of glass, but inside our home, lying curled around my husband in our enormous bed, I felt warm, cozy, and blissfully sated.

We'd be leaving soon to go to my parents' house, where we would spend the night and open presents with the rest of my siblings and their spouses on Christmas morning. Knowing that would be next to impossible to find any alone time with so many people around, we'd chosen to spend the day in bed, fucking, napping, and basically soaking as much of each other up as we could.

My eyes began to droop as Ryan rubbed soothing circles over my back, the sound of his heart beating beneath my ear lulling me to sleep. Just as I started to drift, he spoke softly, and I opened my eyes.

"I thought I was happy. Before. I had the guys at the firehouse who were my friends and I'd spend my free time either hanging out with Joe or fixing up this place. I hoped that someday I'd find someone to love, but for the most part, I was happy," he said.

I laid my hands on his chest and rested my chin there, so I could see him as he spoke. He'd been looking out the window, but he turned his head, tilting his neck so he was gazing down at me. Ryan's fingers sifted through my hair and I leaned into his touch. The look in his eyes was soft and gentle, but I was curious where his train of thought was going.

"But then, I met you and you brought so much light and life and laughter into my world that it was like I'd only been living in shadows before that; like I was finally waking up after a long sleep. That day you showed up at the firehouse with a camera and an apology, that was the day I knew that my life would never be the same again. And I was right." Ryan's lips lifted in a small smile and my heart stuttered in my chest.

"You, Carter Greene, have brought more to my life than I ever thought possible. You've brought laughter and joy, romance and lust, fun and family. You challenge me, drive me crazy and turn my world upside down on a daily basis, but I wouldn't have it any other way because you are my whole world." My vision swam as his words went straight to my heart and I swiped my eyes with my hand. I crawled up the length of him until I hovered just inches from his face and his hands moved to cradle my head.

"Not only did you save me from that fire, you saved me from the path I'd been on. Like you, I thought I was happy, hanging out with my band and having meaningless encounters with complete strangers. I thought that was the life of a rock star and I suppose for some, it is, but it wasn't what I really wanted.

"I grew up with parents who were crazy about each other. I watched Caleb fall in love. I *felt* him falling in love, and I wanted to experience that same feeling for myself, I just never thought it was possible for a guy like me. Then you came into my life, pulling me from the flames, my Superman." I smiled as Ryan rolled his eyes slightly then my face grew serious again. "You are everything to me. You're my best friend, my lover, and my partner in every single thing I do. I cannot imagine taking this journey with anyone else, nor would I want to."

I ended my words with a soft kiss to his lips. Ryan tilted his head, deepening the kiss, and soon he was rolling us both so that he was lying on top of me. I held his stare when he entered me moments later, our bodies speaking for us and our souls strengthening the bond that had been forged long ago.

I winced at the twinge in my ass as I sat down at the island counter in my parents' kitchen a while later, but I had to chuckle when I caught Ryan doing the same. There was no better way to spend a day, in my opinion, than in bed with my husband. But I was grateful that we liked to switch things up or one of us would have been pretty miserable right then. Ryan elbowed me in the side just as Mom asked us how our day had been.

"We just stayed at home and took it easy. It was just what I needed," I answered.

"Me too," Ryan said, his hand coming down to rest on my thigh. I reached under the counter and linked our hands together.

The sounds of several voices filtering in through

the front door had us scrambling from our seats to greet the new arrivals. Emma and her family had arrived at the same time as Micah and Landon and they were all struggling to get their coats off while also holding their overnight bags. Ryan and I rushed forward to help them and I took the pie pan out of Emma's hands. Even though it was covered in foil, I could tell it was freshly baked because it was still warm to the touch. I peered up at her through my lashes and gave her a hopeful grin.

"Yes, twerp. It's blackberry," she said with a laugh. She knew that it was my favorite, so she made it every year.

"What about…"

"Right here. Did you honestly think I'd forget?" she said, holding up a tub of vanilla ice cream. I smiled and leaned forward to kiss her cheek.

"This is why you're my favorite sibling," I announced.

"Ummm, hello! I'm standing right here," Landon complained, and Emma and I both laughed.

"You bring me pie and we'll talk," I teased.

"Manage a guy's entire career and all he wants is pie," Landon muttered jokingly as he started to walk past me. I reached up and tousled his hair, making him scowl at me.

"You know I love you, big guy," I cooed at him, puckering my lips for a kiss. Landon turned and looked at his husband.

"You've been trained to kill with your bare hands, right?" he asked.

"Yeah," Micah answered with a smirk. Landon looked at me and then back at his husband.

"Have at it," Landon deadpanned. With that, he turned and trudged up the steps with their bags.

"No killing over our new carpets. You boys take that stuff outside," Dad joked and we all laughed.

Michelle and her crew showed up next, followed quickly by Caleb and Giovanni. They talked about how slick the roads were on their way over and I was grateful that everyone had made it there safely.

Caleb and Giovanni went to the kitchen to help Mom finish dinner, and I plopped down on the couch next to Ryan and pulled little Ricky onto my lap as we watched *How the Grinch Stole Christmas*. It had always been my favorite of all the animated Christmas specials and even as an adult, I refused to miss it.

"I like that," Ryan whispered in my ear. I gave him a curious look, not sure what he was talking about. "You, holding a kid. Have you ever thought about that?"

"Why, Ryan. Are you asking if I'd consider having kids with you?" I asked sweetly.

"Not now, of course, but maybe…someday?" His tone was hesitant, and I felt myself grin.

"I would love to have children with you. Not just someday, but in the very near future," I answered honestly.

The smile on Ryan's face was nothing short of radiant and it made me want to drag him upstairs and find the nearest private room, so I could have my filthy way with him. I loved him so much and I wanted us to experience every single thing that life had to offer, including having children.

Ryan leaned forward and kissed me, a slow, lingering kiss full of promises. My head was spinning by the time he was done, and he wrapped an arm around my shoulder and pulled me into his side as we continued watching the show. I smiled as I heard the contented sigh that came out of him moments later. *Does life get any better than this?*

Mom called us all to the table just as the cartoon ended and I carried Ricky into the dining room, giving him a kiss on his cheek before handing him off to his father. I sat down next to my husband just as Caleb and Giovanni carried in the last of the platters.

They'd worked with Mom on the menu and

the three of them had gone all out this year. There was ham, turkey, homemade noodles and dressing. Nearly every vegetable imaginable, along with rolls and tiny individual cranberry tarts. It was more food than we'd had in Christmases past, but then again, our family had grown considerably over the last year.

We took turns passing the various dishes around the table until everyone's plates were full and then we dug in. Dinner was filled with lots of laughter and teasing as memories were shared and new ones were made. Of course, there was a lot of talk about Santa's visit that night and whether or not he'd be able to fit the dollhouse Sarah wanted in his sleigh.

After dinner, Ryan, Landon, Micah and I offered to clean up while everyone else went to the living room, so Dad could read *'Twas the Night Before Christmas* to his grandchildren. I smiled at the possibility of him reading that story to our child next year. I looked up as Landon handed me another plate for the dishwasher and caught him wearing the same goofy grin. *Hmm. Maybe there'd be more than one addition to the family.* I was happy for him and Micah. They'd both been through hell and back and they deserved nothing but happiness.

By the time we had cleaned everything up and started the dishwasher, all the kids had been changed into their pajamas and put to bed. Michelle and Jason were the last to walk back downstairs and we all looked at each other. It was completely quiet for a few seconds as we listened to be sure the kids were settled and then we all grinned. It was the moment we'd all been waiting for.

Soon, there was a flurry of activity as we raced to the trunks of our cars to retrieve the multitude of gifts we'd brought. Mom and Dad pulled endless piles of colorfully wrapped gifts out of the hall closet and we took turns placing them all under the tree.

Caleb and I sat on the floor to stuff the stockings for the children while Giovanni wrote out a note to Sarah from Santa, thanking her for the delicious cookies she'd left for him. He stuffed a cookie in his mouth, being sure to leave crumbs on the plate and Caleb and I laughed.

"What? I didn't want her to think Santa didn't like them. It's all about the details," he explained which only made us laugh harder.

We'd just finished filling the stockings with fun little toys and books and hanging them back on the hooks underneath the mantle when Dad and Micah came in from the garage. They were carrying a very elaborate, wooden dollhouse and I heard Caleb gasp beside me.

"Dad, you said you were going to make a doll-house for Sarah, but I never expected something like this," he said.

"It's remarkable," Giovanni added, moving forward to get a better look.

"Eh, it gave me something to do." I could see the pride in Dad's eyes, but as usual, he was modest.

"Don't let him fool you," Mom said, wrapping an arm around her husband's waist and looking up at him adoringly. "He spent hours out in his garage making sure every detail was just right and that there would be no splinters that might hurt Sarah. When he wasn't doing that, he was online, shopping for tiny furniture and a large family of dolls to go with it. If I'm not mistaken, there are the same number of dolls as people in this family," she said with a grin.

"Aww, Dad. You didn't have to go to all that trouble, but thank you. I know she'll love it," Caleb said, walking over to hug our father. Dad hugged him back and then we all got back to work.

It was late by the time we had finished getting everything ready and the dollhouse, along with a couple of other larger items, wrapped for the kids. It had been a busy couple of days and it would be even busier the next day so we all said goodnight and crept quietly up the stairs to go to sleep.

I followed Ryan into my childhood room and shut the door, watching him as he wandered around, touching things and admiring the old posters of popular boy bands from when I was in high school. Ryan had been in my room before on several occasions, but never to spend the night.

"So, have you ever had a boy in your room other than me?" he asked, waggling his eyes at me playfully.

"As a matter of fact, yes. There were numerous occasions," I told him, biting my cheek to keep from laughing as his face fell. "Eventually though, Caleb got his own room and that was the end of that," I ended with a dramatic sigh. Ryan's eyes narrowed and then he picked up a pillow from the bed and hit me in the face with it while I laughed.

"Funny guy," he murmured, but I could see the smile tugging at his lips.

"Come on. Let's hurry up and get changed. I have one other tradition and I want you to come with me."

Ryan gave me a curious look, but then he unzipped our overnight bag and set to work changing into his pajamas. When we both were finished, and had brushed our teeth, I took his hand and led him back downstairs. I didn't bother to turn on any lights as I led him over to my old piano in the corner and pulled out the bench, so we could sit.

I checked the time on my watch.

Midnight.

Perfect.

I ran my fingers over the smooth, black and white keys and closed my eyes. Then, I began to play, just as I did every year, knowing that my mom was smiling in her room. I heard Ryan sigh next to me as he recognized the song, but neither of us said a word as we listened to the gentle chords of "Silent Night" and let the peace and quiet of another beautiful Christmas Eve fill our souls.

CHAPTER
Eleven

Micah

I WOKE, FEELING LIKE SOMETHING WAS OFF. THE bed felt different and the mattress wasn't quite as comfortable as I was used to. I cracked my eyes open and looked around, suddenly remembering where I was and why. A smile stretched my face. My first Christmas with Landon.

I looked over at the man that was asleep next to me. We'd fallen asleep, wrapped around each other, but sometime in the night, he must've gotten too hot because he was on his back with one arm thrown over his eyes and the blanket bunched down around his waist. *Perfect.* I sat up and very carefully pulled the blanket down the rest of the way then lowered myself on top of my husband. Landon's eyes slid open and a lazy grin lifted the corners of his mouth.

"Good morning," he whispered as I began to lay soft kisses along his chin and up his jaw. He turned his head and tried to capture my mouth, but I pulled back, shaking my head at him.

"Not just any morning, baby. Merry Christmas." Landon's eyes opened wider and his smile grew.

"Merry Christmas," he echoed, happily.

"I thought maybe we could enjoy a present all our own before everyone wakes up," I whispered as I resumed kissing him.

"What did you have in mind?" he moaned as my lips trailed down his neck. His breath quickened, and I could feel his rapid heartbeat against my chest.

"I'll do everything, you just lie there and enjoy." I chuckled when he let out a moan. "Oh, and try to be quiet," I reminded him.

Landon lifted his hips, so I could tug his pants down and then I did the same to mine. I pressed him back down against the pillows as I took both our cocks in my fist and began working them up and down. I could hear someone moving around downstairs and I knew we didn't have much time, so I kept up a relentless pace with my hand, swallowing his moans with my kisses.

He whimpered beneath me and I could feel myself nearing the end, so I shifted down the bed and sucked his cock down until it hit the back of my throat. He tasted delicious, like salt and skin and Landon and I moaned with him inside my mouth. I continued stroking my dick, getting myself off to the wanton sounds of my man.

Suddenly, Landon tensed, and his cock grew larger, stretching my lips even farther. His hips lifted off the bed and he let out a strangled cry as his cum filled my mouth and shot down my throat. The taste was enough to send me over the edge and I rested my forehead against his thigh as I shot my seed into my hand. I was still shaking when Landon pulled me up and kissed me then took my hand and licked it clean, sucking on each of my fingers and eliciting a groan.

"Best Christmas present ever!" Landon exclaimed. I chuckled then buried my face into the curve of his neck and let out a contented sigh. He wouldn't be hearing any arguments from me.

We forced ourselves out of bed a few minutes later and headed to the bathroom. After a quick shower together, and brushing our teeth, we wrapped towels around our waists and headed back to our room.

We came to a stop, however, when we ran into Carter in the hallway. I held my breath, waiting for some teasing comment to come out of his mouth about us showering together, but instead, he passed by with barely a glance our way.

"Hey, Carter! What's up? You don't look very good," Landon said, concern lacing his words. I took a closer look and frowned when I saw Carter's pale face. His eyes were wide, and he looked as if he were about to be sick.

"I went downstairs to get some coffee going," he told us.

"What's wrong, Carter? You're starting to scare me," Landon said, reaching for his brother.

"Let's just say...I saw Mommy doing more than...*kissing* Santa Claus," he choked out. Landon and I shared a look and then we were laughing, great wracking laughs that had us doubling over, trying to catch our breath.

"You both suck. I'm going to need therapy for this," Carter grumbled as he walked off, probably to try and find some sympathy from Ryan. Landon and I were still laughing as we made our way to our room to get dressed.

I could smell something delicious cooking as we made our way down the stairs, but we could hear excited chatter coming from the living room, so we headed in that direction. Landon's parents and sisters, along with their husbands and children were there, talking and enjoying cups of coffee while they waited for everyone else to join them. A chorus of "Merry Christmas" rang out as we walked in.

Once everyone was downstairs, we grabbed fresh cups of coffee then gathered around the tree while Rick passed out presents. Sarah was thrilled with the dollhouse and even more excited once she discovered the family that went with it. I watched as she held each figure up to her fathers and gave them a corresponding name of one of her family members.

Ricky and Katherine Elizabeth were still too young to really understand what was going on. The two of them were more interested in the wrapping paper and gift boxes than the toys that were held inside, but they were happy and that was all that mattered.

"I can't wait to have one of those," Landon said quietly from beside me. I looked over and smiled as I saw him watching his nieces and nephew with a sappy grin.

"Who knows. Maybe we'll have one by next year," I mused. Landon turned his head, offering up his lips and I kissed him eagerly. I wrapped an arm around him and he leaned into my side as we continued watching everyone unwrap their presents.

An hour later, the gifts had all been opened and everyone was happy and hungry. We helped lay the food out on the table then dug into the warm cinnamon rolls, fresh fruit, and cheesy sausage and egg casserole as we talked about some of our favorite gifts.

Sarah had beamed when Giovanni opened the coffee mug that she had made for him with her handprint on it. I'd smiled at my best friend as he'd gone on and on about how much he loved it and then kissed his husband and little girl. I could see the emotion in his eyes as he ran his finger over the tiny handprint and then wrapped it back up and laid it gently in its box, as if it were made of the finest china. I knew Giovanni well, and I knew that to him, it was probably even better than that.

Ryan loved the new set of top-of-the-line power tools that Carter gave him, especially when Carter explained that there were plenty of things for Ryan to work on around their house now that they'd be there for more than a few weeks at a time.

Emma and Michelle each loved the spa weekends that their husbands had booked for them and I was touched when Rick gave me his grandfather's old handgun. He explained to me that his grandfather had been a decorated veteran and had used that gun in wartime. I was honored that he would trust me with something so special, but my eyes burned when he told me that rather than sit in an old case, collecting dust, it should be with a member of the family that also served to protect others.

It had been an incredible morning, but one of the best moments was when we presented Rick and Kathy with a gift from all of us along with the words we had chosen to say.

"Mom and Dad, you have always been the most amazing parents," Emma started.

"You've shown us, by your example, what kind of individuals we want to be," Michelle continued.

"You've supported us in all of our decisions," Landon told them.

"You've shown us how to love and be loved," Carter added.

"And you've opened your hearts and your home to not only us, but countless others," Giovanni said.

"Giving all of us a place we could call home," Ryan added.

"And a family we could count on," I said.

"We know that you never got to go on a honeymoon. So, we all pitched in to get you this," Caleb told them, smiling as he handed them the folder.

Kathy already had tears in her eyes as she moved closer to her husband to get a better look, but when he opened the folder, revealing the six-week deluxe European vacation, she broke down in gentle sobs. Rick wrapped his arms around her, but I could tell how moved he was as well by the moisture in his eyes. It was a tender and joyful moment, one that I was sure we would remember as one of our favorites when we relived Christmas memories in the years to come.

After breakfast, we helped clean up the wrapping paper strewn all over the living room floor and then loaded up Kathy and Rick's van and piled into our cars. There weren't many drivers on the road at that time. Most people probably deciding it would be better to stay where they were rather than face the slick roads, but we moved along carefully with one destination in mind.

Matt met us at the door of Agape House with a wide smile and ushered us inside. Morgan and Akio were there as well, and they went with Hudson and Isaac to get the rest of the packages from our cars. When everything was unloaded, we carried them into the dining hall where the kids who lived at the center were gathered.

Lachlan, Rylie, and their two boys arrived as we were handing out the last of the presents and they joined in the fun. We'd all worked at the center long enough and gotten to know the teens quite well, so it hadn't been difficult for us to choose gifts suited to each of their individual interests. Matt kept thanking us over and over again, but the surprised and happy expressions on the kids' faces were all the thanks we needed.

"I'll be right back," I told Landon when my phone buzzed in my pocket. He gave me a curious look, but offered me a quick kiss before I stepped out in the hallway. "Jeremy? What have you got?" I listened for several long moments, firing off questions and listening to his responses. Finally, I hung up and walked back inside.

"Everything okay?" Landon asked when I returned. He'd been talking to Hudson, Matt, and Isaac and I looked at all three of them before saying anything.

"I just got a phone call from one of my men. Jeremy." Hudson stiffened, and I saw Isaac and Matt look at him in concern. Hudson had been in touch with me almost daily, so he recognized the name. "I don't want to get your hopes up too much, things are still too early to tell, but he thinks he may have his first solid lead on locating your brother."

Matt and Hudson's arms went around the younger man as Isaac covered his gasp with a shaking hand, but his blue eyes stayed trained on me. I worried that maybe I should have waited to say anything until I had more information, but then Isaac launched himself at me, hugging me to him.

"Thank you so much, Micah. This is exactly the news I needed to hear today," he said. I looked at Hudson and Matt and saw the tenderness in their eyes and I hugged him back, grateful that I was able to make him happy, but wishing I could do more. I felt badly for the two brothers who had been separated under such terrible circumstances and I was determined that, eventually, I would reunite them.

We spent the rest of the afternoon playing with the kids at the center and paying forward some of the love and happiness we'd all been blessed with. I looked around at the smiling faces, of the kids and the staff and the ones I loved most in the world, and I knew without a doubt that this year had been the best of my life. I had a job I loved, friends and family that would always be there in times of need, and I got to wake up each and every morning in the arms of the most incredible man, my soulmate, my Landon.

As if he'd heard my thoughts, he looked up from across the room and smiled at me. I smiled back, my heart feeling full with just one look from my husband. Life most certainly didn't get any better than that.

EPILOGUE

Kathy

"**M**ERRY CHRISTMAS, MY ANGEL," I heard Rick say.

The smell of freshly brewed coffee teased my senses and made it easier to pry my eyes open. We'd been up late the night before, spreading presents around the tree for our children and grandchildren. Finally, we'd gone to bed, but I'd stayed awake so that I could listen to Carter playing *Silent Night* as soon as it turned midnight. He'd carried on that tradition for many years and it was one of my absolute favorites.

"Merry Christmas, love," I responded, smiling at his handsome face as I sat up in bed and took the steaming mug from his hands.

My husband always did like to spoil me, whether it was bringing me coffee in bed or filling my car with gas so I wouldn't have to. I wasn't the type of woman that needed grand gestures and he knew that. Rick was a man who paid attention to details, who knew that it was the thought you put into the small, everyday things that showed a person how much you cared. I never, for one moment in all our years together, had to doubt his love for me. The man overflowed with it in every word, touch, and look he gave me.

"Did you sleep well?" he asked as he settled onto the bed next to me, leaning his back against the headboard.

"Yes, I did. There's nothing like going to sleep, knowing that everyone you love is safely tucked under the same roof," I answered.

"We're very blessed, aren't we?" Rick said, reaching over to take my hand.

I threaded my fingers through his and held our hands in my lap as we finished our cups of coffee and talked about the day ahead. When we were finished, we each showered and got dressed so we could get downstairs and start breakfast. Rick stopped me before I could leave our room, placing his hands on my waist and turning me around to face him.

"I just need one more minute alone with you," he whispered, nuzzling his face into my neck and causing goose bumps to break out all over my skin. He kissed a line up the side of my neck and onto my chin before finally landing on my lips. I slid my arms around his neck and he held me securely as I melted into him. I was a bit dizzy by the time the kiss ended so it took me a moment to realize what was happening when he slid his hand between us, and opened it to reveal a tiny blue box.

"What's this?" I asked, looking at him in surprise.

"Just a little something I wanted to give you without everyone else around," Rick answered as he flipped the lid open and I let out a gasp at the ring inside.

I reached out and ran a finger carefully over the smooth silver band then pulled it out of its case so that I could see the colorful stones inlaid around it. My eyes welled as I recognized the various birthstones of my entire family.

"I love it," I managed to choke out around my tears. Rick chuckled as he slid it onto my finger.

"You are the one who holds this family together. You give us strength, wisdom, and encouragement, and you've given us all more love than we could have ever imagined. I wanted this ring to be a symbol of the people who love you most in the world because you are our whole world," he said. I reached up to cup his cheek with my hand and noticed tears welling in his own eyes.

"Thank you. I love you so much," I whispered.

Rick held me a few more minutes, resting his chin on my head. I snuggled my cheek against his chest and listened to his heart beating steadily against my ear. It was the perfect way to start the day, enjoying a few quiet moments to ourselves before the chaos took over.

Once everyone got downstairs, we gathered around the tree to open presents. Our family had grown over the past year, with Landon and Micah adopting newborn twins. Spencer and Lilyana had joined our family in the fall and the two fathers were still adjusting to the changes the sweet angels had made in their lives. But, I could honestly say, I'd never seen my son happier.

Carter and Ryan had decided to use a surrogate and were blessed with a little boy, Joseph Caleb Greene, right before Thanksgiving. My other children had all had their share of laughs at the four new fathers' lack of knowledge when it came to newborns, but they'd also pitched in to help as well.

Caleb and Giovanni made sure that their freezers and pantries were stocked and would sit with the babies while the new dads got some rest. Emma and Michelle had shown up at each of their houses with packs of diapers, staying to help fold laundry. That was the thing I loved the most about our family. No matter what was going on in each other's lives, good or bad, we could all count on each other to be there.

I got up and started a fresh pot of coffee and then stood in the doorway as it brewed. Rick came and stood beside me and wrapped his arm around my waist as we watched our children joking and laughing and just enjoying each other's company.

"I am, without a doubt, the luckiest woman in the world," I murmured. Rick grabbed my hand and lifted it, so he could lay a gentle kiss on my wrist.

"I'm not sure luck had anything to do with it," he said quietly. I looked up at him curiously and saw him staring out over our family. "I think it was a mixture of hard work, determination, and compromises. It was knowing when to talk and when it was better to just listen. It was encouraging and strengthening each other and helping each other reach our goals. It was prayer and hope and an abundance of love." Rick looked down at me then and my breath caught in my throat at the look of total adoration in his eyes.

"Each of our children have found the person they belong with in this world, the person who loves them unconditionally and beyond reason. And it all started with you and me. Because we loved each other that way we, in turn, taught our children to love that way also. I can't imagine anyone else that I'd want to be on this epic journey with other than you. You are my best friend, the love of my life, and my soulmate and I thank God every day that you chose me."

My heart felt like it was going to burst with the love I felt for him. Tears streamed down my face and emotion clogged my throat, making it impossible for me to speak, so I raised up on my tiptoes and kissed him instead. His arms went around my waist, pulling me tightly against his body and I melted into his familiar embrace.

"Aw, man!" Michelle whined.

"Get a room!" Landon exclaimed.

"Not in front of the children!" Carter complained, covering Caleb's eyes with his hand. Caleb batted his brother's hand away playfully as we all laughed. Rick and I laughed too as we went over to join our family.

We may be loud, wild, and a bit crazy when we

were all together, but it was just because we loved each other so much. And really, when I thought about it, what more could anyone ask for in their lives than to be loved?

The End

ACKNOWLEDGEMENTS

As always, my first thanks go to my family; my husband, my children, my siblings and my parents. You have stood by my side from the moment I started dreaming up the Greene family. You offered your support, your wisdom and your encouragement and none of this would have become a reality without you. I love you guys. You are my heart and soul.

Thank you, Aimee for your wisdom, your support and your belief in me.

Thank you, Deena for always being someone I can always count on. Your friendship means everything to me and I love you.

Thank you, Jenn for showing me unwavering support, encouragement and friendship. You are the epitome of unconditional love and I don't know what I'd do without you. I love you, PD.

Thank you to my team: Pam Ebeler of Undivided Editing, Jay Aheer of Simply Defined Art, Judy Zweifler of Judy's Proofreading, Stacey Blake of Champagne Formats and my beta readers; Lee Rey,

Melissa McIntyre, Jenn Gibson, Allison Hopfazel (for your work as my PA and editor), Meredith King, Lori Greis, Wendy Lynn, Nemerald and Jodie Temple-Harding. Writing this series has been an amazing journey from beginning to end and I've been very blessed to have the same people working with me and encouraging me throughout the entire process, while adding a few new friends along the way. You all have shown me more support, encouragement and enthusiasm than I could ever repay you for. Thank you all from the bottom of my heart.

ABOUT THE AUTHOR

I am married to my high school sweetheart who let's face it, is a saint for putting up with me all of these years. Together we have been blessed with the chance to raise two amazing human beings and so far we haven't screwed it up; I'll let you know for sure later. I am a business owner and spend more time laughing than actually working most days. I love watching movies, cooking, going to the beach and spending time with my family and best friends. I am an obsessive reader who is a complete sucker for a good love story, but loves to feel a broad range of emotions throughout a book. I think real life is hard enough and so my books offer twists and turns, but always with a happy ending.

I love to hear from my readers. You can reach me at:

Twitter
twitter.com/annabellamicha1

Facebook
www.facebook.com/profile.php?id=100011438515157

Annabella's Sexy Souls
www.facebook.com/groups/233274880449097

Blog
www.annabellamichaels.blogspot.com